INF_ _ _ _ _ _
STORMTROOPERS

ALATHIA MORGAN

CONTENTS

PROLOGUE

RUDI

938-1941 The Gathering Storm

When the war ended—or the Great War, as many called it now—I thought my career was over. All the work I'd done on the dead virus had to be hidden from those who had named themselves "the winners." Though I wasn't sure how it could be considered a win, seeing as there were just as many dead on their side as ours. The only difference was, we'd surrendered.

The stupidity of those in charge had been simply mind-boggling. We could have taken over all of France with my newly infected dead breed.

Not willing to give up on my work, I was forced to move my experimentations to my own laboratories, being built underground on my parents' estate.

With so many of our leaders and scientists tasked with peacetime theories, I took one of the few positions offered to me at the university. Starting out as a lowly assistant, word of my achievements had spread, making me a well sought-after expert in my field to teach fresh new minds.

Unable to talk about my personal research, I continued to give lectures, as well as a few classes, on the ways in which our bodies were susceptible to disease. When an exceptionally bright student would begin to ask questions regarding my work, they were invited to one of my weekly dinners, where the discussions weren't monitored.

Karl Müller had stayed on with me as my personal butler, but was actually a lab assistant who couldn't be replaced. He would go out and gather people—ones who would never be missed—to test on in my underground labs.

We'd had to excavate and build sites so our testees wouldn't be able to infect us or other humans until we were ready for them. Once the workers completed our lab, they would be expendable and would be used as our first test subjects.

It wasn't like we could leave people alive who knew about what we were doing and where we were doing it. Though it sounded as if I was trying to hide something, that wasn't necessarily the case. The reality of it was, I didn't want my other associates to get wind of what I was working on. They would no doubt steal and take the credit for my creations, and that was something I couldn't let happen under any circumstances.

The subject of biology and how viruses spread were simply fascinating to me. I'd managed to put my time for studying—as the mass renovations under my home continued—to good use.

I intended to create the perfect weapon for my country to use: The Superhuman Storm Troopers. They would be alive, and stronger than any normal soldier. It was going to take time and patience to accomplish my goals, but I was willing to make the sacrifices needed to fulfill the dream of a German nation that would tell our "winners" to take a hike.

· · · ● ●· ● ● ●· ·

The Pentagon, Washington D.C.

Joseph Fitzgerald

Rumblings had come out of Europe that the Germans were gearing up for a new war. This was the one thing that kept me up at night, as I contemplated on how to deal with the dead coming back to life.

When I'd returned home from the war, I hadn't let the horror stop me from working hard to prepare in case something like it happened again. The world had changed in an instant when the dead had risen to walk among the living. With the help of a rare survivor I'd tracked down, I began testing his blood to formulate a vaccine that could save our country if we ever had to go through another war such as that in the future.

It had taken years for the government to approve testing on human beings, so I'd had to work hard to make more of the actual virus that caused the outbreak to begin with. Only those with a high security clearance had been allowed in the test areas, due to the dangerous nature of my work. Once we had the needed results, all the virus samples were destroyed, with the exception of the original, and a few others I'd kept hidden in case they were needed.

It wasn't until after I was betrayed by Vivianne, a female spy, that I realized just how dangerous the virus was. I couldn't risk someone working for an enemy getting their hands on it to use against innocent people, so I took precautions by hiding the virus samples in a place where no one would ever think to look, leaving special instructions for my children on where to find them if I died. At the moment, they had no idea anything of this magnitude existed.

Sweat dripped down my forehead as we prepared to let a few of the infected out to bite those subjects who were dying. They'd agreed to do this, having only days, if not hours, to live. They'd signed all the legal forms and documents before being placed into comas, allowing for their families to receive the compensation for their services.

With a nod, two soldiers took hold of the infected, secured in a straight-jacket, and led it to the nearest bed.

The infected wasted no time in trying to get a bite out of the soldier who'd removed its mouth guard with his gloved hand. Then, forcing its head down, it gnawed into the unconscious man's arm. The soldiers, careful not to get near the teeth, yanked the infected off and directed it to the bed of the next subject.

There were ten test subjects in total: five had been given the vaccine, and five hadn't. Once the infected had finished with the tenth person, it was removed from the room to be put down. Jumping into action, we took blood from each of our test subjects, ready to evaluate how the virus mutated.

As much as I hated it, there wasn't really a more humane way to conduct these experiments. For many years, I'd been instructed that we could only test on animals. While that would give us some results, those poor things couldn't give their consent, having no idea what we were doing to them.

It wasn't like we could put them back out into the wild after the tests were done. If we'd done that, something much worse could have come of it.

The ethical and moral questions continued to plague me, but if this virus was unleashed on the human race, we would need a way to combat it, so it felt as if the ends justified the means.

Now, we waited to see the end results. We had taken extra precautions by strapping them down to their beds in case they turned into the infected when they died.

Hours later, the verdict was in: my study was a failure.

Over half of those we injected with the vaccine still turned when they died. The reports weren't going to be the glowing conclusions I needed to keep the funding coming in for our study.

I sank to the floor with my head in my hands. We needed to come up with something that worked, because war was just on the horizon. The president hadn't declared it, but it was only a matter of time before the Germans sank one of our ships, plunging us into the start of the Second World War.

The pressure continued to mount; I had nothing to show for all my years of hard work. I would need to go back to the drawing board, hoping that a miracle was just around the corner.

CHAPTER ONE

—·—

CAMERON

DECEMBER 1941 – MAY 1942

The drill sergeant started yelling as soon as I'd gotten off the bus. What I didn't know then was that he never, ever stopped.

I was certain his voice had replaced that of my mother's, because he was in my dreams again. Suddenly, I woke with a start. He was yelling at us.

"Fall out! We've been attacked!" His voice filled the bunkroom, spurring all of us into action.

As we raced out the door, rifles in hand, I could see all the barracks emptying out, with soldiers running across the dusty road to the main area.

I jogged up behind the others. "What happened?"

"He said something about an attack, which is why we're all carrying rifles," Pope Wilson called out to me over his shoulder.

"Wouldn't we hear someone shooting at us?"

Pope only shrugged in response.

"Ten-hut!" We immediately stood at attention. It was habit now, but a few weeks ago, we'd been a slow, disorganized crew.

"We have just received word that our navy was attacked by Japanese bombers on the Hawaiian Naval Base in Honolulu. We don't have the casualties list yet, as this just happened, but all bases have been put on alert in case they try to attack us again. Most of you have finished the majority of your training, which is why there will be a special ceremony this afternoon. It is very possible we'll be shipping out in the next few days to wherever we're needed. As soon as we have updates, we'll post them. Effective immediately, all leave has been canceled, and we will remain vigilant. Shifts have been drawn up to keep a lookout for planes. Ask your platoon leaders for further instructions. Dismissed!"

"Oh my God, can you believe it? How could this happen to our troops?" Pope rambled on from beside me. "Do you think we'll go to war? I mean, the president has to let us go after them, right? Someone needs to pay."

I frowned, contemplating the ramifications of what this attack could mean. "Yeah, I guess so. I think that's where my brother's stationed."

"Hope he was able to shoot down a couple of those Japs," he snickered, mimicking shooting planes out of the sky.

A chill ran down my spine. We'd just spent weeks being trained on how to kill another human being, but things had gotten real, and fast. To be honest, I hadn't really thought it through, that I would actually have to do it someday.

• • • • ● • ● ● ● • •

The training camp took on a feeling of anticipation and excitement as things moved in the direction of assignments to units that would soon ship out to Europe.

Hastily erected lookout towers were completed swiftly, allowing for us to search the empty skies for planes that might possibly fly overhead.

The excitement also brought out the newness of our unit, and the fact that we weren't quite battle ready. False alarms happened frequently, though in the mass confusion, only two privates actually fired their weapons.

Since they were already lowly privates, their ranks couldn't be stripped further. The camp had latrines that needed to be dug, so that was their punishment. Needless to say, they were going to be expert diggers by the time we shipped out.

As we'd been given physicals before entering into the army, we were now being ordered to report for more vaccines, along with attending a lecture discussing the dangers we would come across on the battlefield.

"We're unsure if these dead things will be used again during the fighting," the instructor advised in a calm voice, seeming unconcerned. "But you must be prepared in case this happens to you or other members of your unit. There were only a few cases in the last war, and while we don't want to alarm you, there's a good possibility the Germans may try to use it again, as it is a modern means of psychological and biological warfare."

"You're saying our fellow platoon members are going to try to kill us?" Pope called out, causing all of us to laugh. "Isn't that what happened when Private Jones's gun went off last night?"

"Not exactly, Private Wilson. But if you'd like to join him on latrine duty, I'm sure that can be arranged." The instructor's eyebrow moved upward, waiting for him to speak again. "Ah, nothing else to say? Well, then, let us continue. Basically, the situation we encountered could only be remedied by the use of toxic mustard gas. It would melt the flesh from the bodies, so they couldn't move or sink their teeth into you. If you begin to see your dead companions move, or hear their death rattle, proceed with caution." He glanced toward Privates Booth and Anderson, as if they would be the ones to shoot first.

"We don't want you to harm those who are simply injured. This is merely an exercise in caution. You all will receive the vaccine, which should prevent you from rising from the dead. Hopefully, this will put a kink in the

German's plans, as they don't know we have this available. Any other questions will have to be shelved, because we honestly have no idea what we're working with at this point." He nodded toward the team of medics and nurses waiting to give us the vaccine.

"This is not to be discussed with anyone outside of those in this room. We don't need to cause a panic amongst the civilians for something that hasn't happened, or may never even occur."

Pope groaned beside me. "Great, we're getting shots from male nurses. Where's the incentive in that?"

"Hey, I'd watch what you say, or the instructor might change his mind and put you on latrine duty." I shifted away from him, just to make sure I didn't look to be a part of whatever he brought upon himself.

"Nah, he wouldn't do that." He glanced around nervously, making sure he hadn't been heard.

I grinned. "You know he would. And I wouldn't want to take a chance like that, considering the alternative. You'd be up to your elbows in shit."

• • • ● ● • ● ● ● • •

It was the middle of January before we were sent to the coast to board one of the first ships available to transport troops across the ocean.

While it was a long, crowded journey, I was itching to fight the enemy. We'd been training day and night, so the sudden halt of activity didn't sit well with the four hundred men gathered in such an enclosed space with nothing to do but think.

I had to laugh when Pope joined some of the others in kissing the ground when we finally stepped onto British soil, as several of them hadn't taken too well to the rolling motion of the boat. It would take at least a few days for them to get their land legs back again.

"Better watch out, or I'm going to send my first letter home to your girl, telling her you aren't the big, tough man you pretend to be," I teased, seeing the color slowly coming back into his cheeks.

"Hurry to the dining hall. We'll need to give you instructions to make sure you keep all the blackout regulations while you're here in Britain," a lieutenant bellowed to move us along. "For those of you who weren't aware, all windows must be covered and panels are to remain over doors so that there aren't any lights to guide the Germans to us. The air raids will begin in less than two hours, and we must have you all situated before it starts."

"Air raids? That doesn't sound very sportsmanlike of the Germans to drop bombs on us. We just got here," Pope joked, but I heard the fear behind the statement.

"You didn't know? They've been bombing here on a regular basis since August 1940. It's been talked about by some of the boys as we've gotten closer to the action on this side."

"That would be awful to come all this way just to get taken out by a bomb," Jerry Crum scoffed in disgust.

"We're going to be sitting ducks if we don't get a move on, that's for sure," I prodded, increasing my pace.

"Next thing you know, they'll have us filling sandbags instead of shooting the enemy." Pope retorted, moving a little faster as well.

Little did we know that filling sandbags was about the only thing we could do for the next few months until the Allied commanders decided where they were going to send us next.

Letters from home kept up the morale in between running into buildings, helping the city of London put out fires. Though we were only infantry, our unit was one of the few that volunteered to help out instead of sitting on our rears in the camp, waiting for the next plane to fly overhead and drop a load of bombs upon us.

This wasn't the war I'd imagined when I signed on, or when they said we were going to be shipped overseas, but it looked like we were going to be one of the first groups to be sent down to Northern Africa to help keep the Germans at bay until we could gain enough ground for an invasion of France.

Pope wasn't the only one complaining about another trip across open seas, but this time, we would hug the shorelines so that subs would be less likely to find us.

· · ● ● ● · ● ● ● · ·

"All hands on deck!" The words rang up and down the length of the ship, causing everyone to frantically run.

I hadn't felt anything hitting us, but maybe I wouldn't know since I wasn't in the Navy. Although, I was pretty sure we would've felt something if there were torpedoes being shot at us. Maybe we were just taking extra precautions to avoid having that happen.

Just the day before, one of the ships in our fleet had sunk with a full crew on board. In fact, we were approaching that same area, so we might be searching for survivors.

"Any idea what's going on?" I asked a crewman, scanning the area with a pair of binoculars.

"We've lost two boats in this area, and we're making sure they don't get ours as well," he answered politely.

Even though we were all in the same military forces, the navy and the army didn't really see eye to eye on things. To most of the navy guys, we were just useless passengers that were taking up space on their boat.

Off in the distance, I spotted something floating on the water.

"There! Isn't that a lifeboat?" I pointed toward the left, because I had no clue which was starboard or port, or whatever.

He turned, focusing on the area.

"All stop! I repeat, all stop!" he yelled as he ran over to ring the bell on the side of the boat.

I stood back, out of the way, as several sailors ran up, taking turns looking through the binoculars.

"It's a life raft. Send down one of ours, and let's see if we've got any survivors," the commanding officer ordered.

Within minutes, they had lowered a few dinghies with small motors rushing toward the small raft. The ship had come to a stop as we waited for them to return.

As word spread that a lifeboat had been spotted, more of my unit appeared up on deck.

"What's happening?"

"Are we being attacked?"

"Is someone in that boat?"

Not really knowing the answers, I watched from the railing as the boat got closer. It was hard to tell what was happening out there in the darkness, and we couldn't shine any lights due to German's discovering us.

The boats finally pulled up to the side of the ship with the small raft. It was full of soldiers, as well as a few women.

We all made way for them to climb up onto the deck. Since I was close to the ladder, I caught a glimpse of the most beautiful women I'd ever seen. Even with the filth and grime she'd acquired while being stranded in a raft, she looked amazing.

As if by some unspoken word, everyone followed them to the mess hall, impatiently waiting for answers as they were given warm bowls of soup and fresh water. Medics did quick assessments on those who weren't seriously injured before allowing them to eat and rehydrate.

"Can you tell us what happened?" the captain questioned them.

"We were on the ship when it suddenly exploded. We only had a few minutes to grab one of the rafts before the ship sank. We picked up as many of the injured as we could, but there were so many out there who needed to be rescued," the pretty brunette explained in a quiet tone.

In the light of the ship's interior, she still held a classic beauty, but the lines under her eyes spoke of the horrors she'd experienced in just the past twenty-four hours.

When the captain had gathered all the particulars of their ordeal, he began to dismiss everyone, when a voice from the back called out, "If I'd known the army had women in the ranks, I'd have joined a long time ago. You ladies are welcome to share my bunk with me."

"That will be enough!" the captain roared, glaring at all of us. "These women joined the service to help their country, not become your personal attendants. You will treat them with the same respect you would your mothers and sisters. If I hear of anyone making those types of remarks again, you'll be scrubbing the decks with your own toothbrush. Is that clear?"

"Yes, sir," we all responded.

"See that they're given clean uniforms and placed in my quarters. I'll bunk with the XO until we reach port. If you ladies need anything, please, let me know."

"Thank you for your generosity, Captain. Honestly, I think beyond dry clothes and checking on the wounded, we just need to sleep," the brunette replied.

I didn't know where they would be sent after we docked, but I could only hope I'd see more of her. I sincerely wanted to meet her, as did the other twelve hundred or so men on board, making my chances seem minimal.

The idea of going to war was looking better. I felt I could handle any kind of battle if it meant being near an angel like her.

Chapter Two

Irene

December 7, 1941

P earl Harbor has been attacked...The U.S. is at war with Japan.

Every radio in every shop blared the story as we walked home from church.

"It's finally happened. There'll be no stopping this war," my father, Joseph, groaned, as he took a seat at the table.

He'd been a surgeon during the Great War. The horrors of that time had propelled him to become a scientist, to help create a cure in case the Germans ever unleashed their secret weapon again.

Emma Fitzgerald gave him a stern look as she helped our maid bring out the food from the kitchen.

"Joseph, don't scare the children. There will be plenty of time to talk about the war in the coming days." She glanced pointedly at my brothers and sisters, who were staring at him wide-eyed.

"You're right, dear. Everything will be all right," he belatedly tried to reassure us.

"Mother, would you mind if I ran over to the Bush's house after lunch? I'd really like to see if they have any news about Drew." As the oldest, I had a little more freedom than my siblings, but I didn't want my family to worry about me.

"Of course, dear. I'm sure they're just as concerned with this news as the rest of us. Do you know where he's stationed yet?" She took her seat, slightly out of breath from rushing to get everything out while it was still warm.

"No. I'm worried that he was sent to Pearl Harbor."

"They wouldn't allow them to give out his destination, then?" Pop asked.

"Unfortunately, they didn't. He promised to write or call when they got there, but it was very hush-hush." I tried not to think about the implications of what it might mean.

"You should be there with his mother in case they hear something. If it gets too late, I'll have your father stop over to escort you home."

"Really, Mama, I'll be fine," I protested. I'd been walking all over the city for years now.

She beamed in his direction. "Yes, but it will give him a reason to come home on time."

I hated leaving Mama at home with only the children to keep her company, but I couldn't help it. No one knew that Drew had proposed before he'd left for boot camp, and simply calling his family wasn't going to lessen my worry.

Drew's sister, Rebecca, and I, had been friends for years. If there was anyone who could be trusted with my secret, it was her.

My steps increased as I imagined all the horrible things that could happen to him.

While our homes were only ten blocks apart, it seemed like a completely different place, as the houses grew smaller and closer together.

This part of Washington was safe, but I could see people were already sending worried, suspicious glimpses at their neighbors.

With a soft knock, I stood at the Bush's door.

When it opened, Rebecca threw herself into my arms. "He's got to be all right, doesn't he?" she sobbed as I led her inside.

"Of course he's okay. He couldn't have made it to Pearl Harbor yet," I assured her, knowing it was quite possible he was already there.

She wiped at her eyes, taking a seat next to her mother. "See, Mama? Even Irene thinks he's okay. We've got to stay positive until they tell us otherwise." She then turned her attention to me. "Father went to see what he could find out. Since this is Washington, I'm sure there'll be tons of rumors, with a little bit of the truth mixed in."

"Yes, that's true. Pop went straight to the lab, so we probably won't see him for several days." I frowned. "You'd think as long as he's been working on vaccines for our soldiers, he'd be happy it was finally going to be tested. Instead, he seemed almost nervous, thinking he hadn't done enough."

"His work is classified, isn't it?" Rebecca asked, trying to bring her mother into the conversation.

I shrugged. "Mostly. We know some of what he does, but a few things he works on are confidential. Part of working for the government, I guess."

"Could he find out where Drew is?" Mrs. Bush's head popped up with the hopeful thought.

"Um, I don't think he has access to that kind of information. He works with test tubes and viruses. I'm sorry. But if we find out anything, I'll be sure to let you know," I promised.

There was a sinking pit in the bottom of my stomach as the hours continued to pass with no word from the West Coast. Even if Drew was among the dead, it might take days before his family was notified, considering the number of casualties they were dealing with. Those who were still alive and able were going to be hard-pressed to help the wounded before collapsing from exhaustion themselves.

About thirty minutes before dark, I stood and hugged Mrs. Bush.

"I'd better be heading home before it gets too late. You make sure to call me if you find out anything. The longer it is without any word, the better." I hoped that was the truth.

Rebecca stood as well, giving me a crushing embrace before handing me my coat. "Be safe out there."

Giving her a weak smile, I left and headed toward home.

The sun was sinking fast, leaving gorgeous streaks of orange across the sky, mixed with an ominous golden red.

Nothing would ever be the same. We'd been attacked on U.S. soil, and now it was time to fight.

· · · · ● ● · ● ● · ● · ·

Two days later, the news came. Drew was gone.

Rebecca could barely speak through her tears, while her mother wailed in the background.

"We'll be right there." I clutched the small plastic ring he'd given me that I'd placed on my necklace. The one he had proposed to me with until he could get me the real thing.

Mama came bustling into the room. "Who was that, dear?" She took one look at my face and knew. "Oh, no. He's gone?"

I rushed into her arms and let the tears fall. Drew, and I had been best friends for years with the hopes of something more, but now that was all gone.

"I can't tell you that it's not going to hurt, but one day, it won't hurt as much," she comforted, letting me get it all out. "There, now. Are you ready to go over?"

"Yes," I answered, swiping a few more tears away. "I'll go powder my nose and meet you back here."

When I returned, she was holding a casserole dish. Mama was always prepared for whatever might happen. If only I could be as good of a wife...

"Come, dear." She took my arm and bustled me out to the car.

In a fog, we made our way to their house and up the steps to what felt like the end of the world.

We weren't the only ones who had heard the news. Poor Rebecca was having a hard time comforting the mourners showing up and attending to her devastated mother as well.

Without a thought, I slid my coat off and took charge of those coming to the door, while Mama headed to the kitchen to organize the food.

The line seemed endless until school let out, and everyone dispersed to gather their children. As the last person made their way out the door, I turned to Rebecca.

"Go lie down. It'll help if you're rested for this evening," I ordered.

"I won't be able to sleep," she protested, but headed toward the room she shared with her younger sisters. "Oh, God. They'll be home soon, and I'll have to tell them…"

"No, I'll do it." Wrapping my arm around her shoulders, I led her into the room and sat her down on the bed. The doctor had left something to help them calm Mrs. Bush, so I gave Rebecca a much smaller dose. "They'll need you tonight and in the morning."

"Are you sure?" she murmured as she drifted off.

"I'm sure. Rest. I'll be here when you wake up."

Closing the door, I took a deep breath, willing the tears not to fall. There wasn't time to mourn right now. I could do that later when I wasn't needed to keep things going.

• • • ● ●• ● ● •• •

Exhausted, and with nothing left to give, I dragged myself into the house, planning to collapse into bed as soon as I could. The mourners continued visiting all evening, and had finally left the family in peace sometime after eleven.

With my hand on the curve of the staircase, I spied the newspaper sitting on the table where Pop had put it when he'd finished with it. Drawn by the words splashed across the front, I found myself walking toward it.

Calling all women to help release a serving man for combat duty. Congress approves the formation of the

WAACs to relieve men for active duty during this time of war.

"Hmm, looks like they learned a few things from the Great War, after all. At least you'll be paid and connected with the army instead of being classified as a civilian, like we were."

Mama looked up at me. "Oh, Irene. You want to go, don't you?"

"Yes," I replied softly. The black hole that had been growing inside of me over the past few hours lessened a bit at the thought of helping to save someone else's fiancé.

"Your father won't like it, but you're a grown woman, and have the college education this requires." She looked around to make sure Pop wasn't somewhere close by, listening. "I'd apply, and if you're accepted, he won't have much to say about it, seeing as it would be a done deal." She smiled. "Tomorrow. There will be enough time to take care of it tomorrow."

"You're right." I nodded wearily, clutching my necklace like a lifeline. "Good night."

• • • ● ● • ● ● • •

I'd applied the next day, then had to wait anxiously to find out if I was accepted. The morning of Drew's funeral, it arrived just as we were about to walk out the door.

The note burned a hole in my pocket throughout the funeral. It wasn't until after the meal that I was finally able to sneak off to Rebecca's room for a moment to myself.

We are pleased to inform you that you have been accepted into the Officer's Training Classes for the Women's Army Auxiliary Corps. We expect you to join your class on the following Monday to begin training as soon as possible.

Rebecca walked in and joined me. "I thought I saw you sneak off a few minutes ago. What's you got you so excited?" She took a seat next to me and started reading over my shoulder. "Oh, my gosh. You signed up? They've already accepted you?" she squealed quietly, giving me a fierce hug before slapping my arm. "Are you absolutely out of your mind?"

I laughed, glad I could still find humor in something now that Drew was gone.

"Yes, and no. I'm not crazy."

She frowned. "Why would you do this? It won't bring him back."

"It won't, but I feel like this is the best way for a woman to fight those who attack us. Can I do a lot or actually fight? No. But I'll be letting someone who can go to the front. We're going to need all the people we can get to make sure this threat is taken care of, so more of our boys can come home." As I spoke the words out loud, I realized this was the best way I could honor Drew.

"You know he wanted to marry you, right?"

Smiling, I pulled out the necklace with his ring on it. "Yes. We were going to be married when he came home. Now, I'll always have something to remember him by."

She threw her arms around me. "I knew it! He wouldn't say anything before he left, but in his last letter, he asked me to take care of you like a sister, so I hoped he'd spoken to you about it." Releasing me, she holds me at arm's length. "It'll be hard to let you go, but I get it. I wish that was in the cards for me as well. You'll have to write and keep in touch so we don't worry about you."

"I'll do my best. They'll probably send me to some godforsaken place to type up requisition forms."

I'd heard all my mama's stories, and knew it wasn't going to be that easy.

· · · ● ● · ● ● · · ·

"No, I won't let her go." Pop tossed the letter back at me in anger. "Did you learn nothing from the funeral we attended today? Drew died, and he didn't even get a chance to fight. It was senseless."

"That's exactly why I have to do this, Pop. I have to make sure more of our men come home to their families. They're not going to send women into battle," I reasoned.

"Right, like they didn't send your mother into combat? Those bombs that fell on our camp were pretty real." He sank into the closest chair. "I could get you a position at my lab where you would be away from the danger."

"You mean where you could keep an eye on me? I understand you want to keep me safe, but it's time I got out on my own. I've finished college, and was going to work until Drew came back. Now, the thought of doing that in the same place we fell in love would be too difficult."

"Oh, honey." Mama patted my hand in sympathy. "I think this will be a good thing for you. When do you leave?"

"I have to be at Ft. Des Moines on Monday." I held out the list that had accompanied the letter.

She took it with a smile. "I remember trying to get these items before I shipped out. We'll go shopping first thing in the morning. They don't tell you all the little comforts you'll miss when you're on an army base."

A voice cleared at the opening between the parlor and the dining room.

"She's not the only one who signed up. I ship out on Sunday as well," my younger brother, Luke, announced.

"Not you too?" Pop groaned. "You have no idea what the Germans are capable of. They've had over twenty years to come up with more horrors they're hoping to unleash on our unsuspecting army."

"We know, Pop. You've told us about some of them, but we want our chance to fight. The Japanese just came over here and killed our people. It's time to take the fight overseas. I'm joining the Airforce."

With tears in her eyes, Mama gave each of us a hug. "We are so proud of you both. Your father just wants you to be safe. Now, come on. We have to have a going away party and there's tons to do."

"She's right. I'm proud of you." He stood and saluted us. "There's something you both need to know before you leave, though."

Mama nodded in approval as he walked toward his office, not waiting for us to follow him.

Once inside his office, he closed the door before turning to face us.

"What I'm about to tell you is classified, and you can't share it with anyone unless your lives are in danger." Taking our seats, he told us a story that seemed so unbelievable. "When the dead began to rise..."

CHAPTER THREE

— · —

IRENE

Officer training wasn't much different from what I'd expected, and I passed with flying colors. I'd volunteered to be sent to Florida to work with the Aircraft Warning Service, or AWS. It felt like the right move, because my brother was going to be one of the pilots. While I probably wouldn't get to bring his plane in, I still felt a connection to him.

It was liberating to know that the planes flying overhead were about to play an important part in the war effort. Even though we weren't supposed to know where they were being sent, there were always a few of our group that were in the know.

The thing that continued to plague me the most were the words my father had spoken just days before we'd left. It was all I could do not to inquire about the truth of his words.

"Irene, Luke, our family has a history with this specific type of warfare. Most of the time, it's given another name so that others won't understand the magnitude of what happened or could happen again."

I frowned at his secretive actions. "Pop, what are you talking about?"

"I'm talking about the dead who come back to life and infect the living. Somehow, the infection, or virus, that destroyed the Titanic was discovered by the Germans. I'm pretty sure a spy stole it from me, but that's beside the point. They were able to infect living things and turn them loose on our soldiers. Once the infection takes hold, the dead begin to attack the living trying to eat them."

"They eat them?" I asked in horror.

"They did. I'd had just enough warning and was able to keep it from spreading all over France. The only way these things can be killed is to shoot them in the head. If someone's bitten, the only way to keep them from turning is if they have a natural immunity built up or have been vaccinated. We call it the ZIV vaccine, and nobody really explains why it's given to all our soldiers. It's keeping our own from rising from the dead and attacking our troops," Pop explained, trying to keep from getting too detailed with all the science behind it.

"I'm telling you both, so if something like this starts to happen, you can help keep it from spreading." He wrung his hands in anguish. "I've been working twenty years to come up with a vaccine that will keep our troops safe, but I'm certain the Germans have also been working against us to make an even worse version of the weapon. We know they don't have any issue using humans for some of their experiments, so please, be safe out there."

We'd both nodded, trying to wrap our minds around the concept of the dead coming back to life. It sounded like something from a comic book that my little brothers would read.

Now, here in the air control tower directing traffic, I couldn't help but think of all the ways a virus like this could be used against us. If the general population knew about it, they would start killing innocent citizens, no matter how much they were cautioned against it. Even now, those of German or Japanese ancestry were being forced to relocate to camps so they wouldn't start attacking us on our own soil.

While I personally thought it was stupid to take families from their homes, I understood the suspicion and fear that made it possible for that to happen.

As I was contemplating the fate of the world, one of our air officers stuck his head around the door. "Officer Fitzgerald?"

"Yes, sir." I stood and saluted him.

"They've requested that you report to Director Hobby's temporary office immediately. Leader Graham will take over until you return."

"Sir, do you know what this is about?" I hesitated, because this wasn't going to be good news.

Lifting an eyebrow, he shrugged in answer to my question. "They'll tell you all about it when you arrive. I was just asked to have you report and make sure your shift was covered."

"Yes, sir." I hurried past him and down the narrow stairs from the tower to the ground. It was much noisier outside the tower, with planes landing and taking off. Our headphones managed to keep some of the excess noise that the tower walls couldn't keep out.

Not wanting to keep anyone waiting, I hurried straight to the director's temporary office. She'd come to the base a few days ago, making sure we were all behaving in a manner that befitted women of the corp.

I smoothed my hair, hoping to remove any wisps that had escaped. With a loud knock, I opened the door and entered into the call center.

"Third Officer Fitzgerald, reporting as directed, ma'am." I stood at attention, waiting for her response.

"At ease, Officer." She motioned toward the empty chair as she walked over to close the door. "Please, have a seat."

Repositioning herself behind the desk, she looked me up and down.

"General Eisenhower has requested a few select members of our corps to accompany the soldiers throughout Europe. He's looking for French speakers, and you were one of two who had put that down on your application. How good would you say your French is these days, Officer?"

"Mon Français est excellente," I replied in French.

"Very good. You learned from your mother, who was one of the few women in the Signal Corps, correct?"

"Yes, ma'am. My father was a surgeon on the front during the Great War."

"Hmm..." she hummed, appearing to look at something in my file. "I'll be recommending you to accompany a few others who have been selected to help General Eisenhower. There's a ship sailing to Great Britain in two days. Until then, and while on board, you will be training in other secretarial duties he may need you for while under his command. Is there any reason I shouldn't send you over there?" Her appraisal seemed to suggest I might have something that would need to be disclosed to her.

"No, ma'am." The words of my father ran through my head about the dead that might try to attack us.

"Very well. I like to make sure all of our women have volunteered before being sent overseas. We don't have many who know French, so the list is short for those we can use. I'll expect you to have the same good manners and decorum for which you've shown while here in Florida." She stood and held out her hand.

I nodded as I reached out to shake it. "Yes, ma'am. I'll do my best."

"We're counting on you. The more women we have working during this war will prove to everyone just how valuable we are to the war effort. Make us proud." With those words, I was dismissed and fled the room, but didn't get far.

"Ah, I see you've accepted the director's offer. Now, if you'll come with me, we'll get you outfitted for your journey. Do you have a preference for skirts only, or are you willing to wear slacks?" the director's assistant questioned as the door to the inner office shut behind me.

"I'm sure wearing skirts would be fine for an official occasion, but if I'm to accompany the general, I wouldn't want the men to whistle at my clothing options." I smiled, perfectly willing to conform to the conditions of war by wearing slacks.

She offered me a smile. "Very wise. Diving into a trench to avoid an air raid isn't really time for wearing skirts."

"My job is to help the general, not flirt with men who only see me as a skirt." I wasn't going overseas to find a husband, for goodness' sake. After all, I'd just lost my fiancé.

"Very well. I'll have everything ready for you. Until departure, you're relieved of your duties here. The air officer has been informed, and a replacement is en route. Good luck, Officer Fitzgerald." She saluted me, then turned on her heel, hurrying off to the next problem that needed to be solved.

· • • ● ●• ● ● •• ·

"Mama?" I cried into the phone. "It's Irene, and I'm being moved. It's the same kind of situation as yours when you were in the Signal Corps."

"Oh, Irene. They're not going to let you come home first?" she asked, letting me know she understood where I was going, and that I couldn't tell her any of the details.

"It's a great opportunity, and I'm so glad you wanted me to learn French. It will come in handy where I'm going. I'll write as often as I can," I promised.

"Your father will be so disappointed he didn't get to speak to you before you go. I'll give him and the others your love. Be safe and remember what your father told you. It's part of our family legacy to make sure it doesn't happen again," she instructed.

"I understand, Mama. What are you doing these days?" I wanted to speak to her for just a little bit longer, knowing it would be the last time for a while.

Mama enthusiastically gave me all the details. "All the ladies of the neighborhood have volunteered to help with the war effort in some manner. I even got Mrs. Bush to come with me to one of the meetings, and she's agreed to knit socks for the soldiers going overseas."

I giggled quietly, imagining the soldiers in Africa and the Pacific needing thick socks in the sweltering heat. "I'm sure they'll appreciate it."

"Your father has insisted we start a small garden out here in the yard, so we'll have vegetables in case things get bad."

"I'm sure it won't come to that, but fresh vegetables are always welcome." I grinned at the way some things stayed the same, no matter the fact that a war was going on.

"Mama, I've got to go, but tell everyone I miss them, and that I promise to write."

"Be careful, dear. Remember to duck when the bombs start to fall."

"Will do. Bye, Mama." I brushed at the tear sliding down my face. I was a WAAC, and it wouldn't do to show tears falling in public.

• • • ● ● • ● ● • •

Dear Mama,

You're never going to believe the number of things that have happened to us in just the past few days. We were put on a boat being sent to London, but upon arrival, were immediately transferred to another ship to report to our assignment farther south.

I was one of the few who were blessed to not get seasickness, but others of our group weren't as lucky, so we were standing on deck for some fresh air when our ship was torpedoed. They actually hit our ship!

Needless to say, being thrown into a raging sea wasn't my idea of a grand adventure.

A few of us were able to get into a lifeboat, where we helped rescue others drifting in the sea. A battleship transferring soldiers happened to be close by and came to our rescue. We arrived at our destination, slightly bedraggled, but alive.

If that is the closest to the horrors of war I get, then I'll be just fine. I'm afraid it's just the beginning of the stories I'll one day be telling to my children, though.

Really, there's no need to worry. We are safe on land, and I couldn't be happier. They are going to keep us busy, and for that, I'm thankful. Anyway, I was sure Pop would have heard about our adventures, and I wanted to make sure you had my side of the story.

Lots of Love,

Irene

CHAPTER FOUR

‒ · ‒

THEA

BERLIN, GERMANY

I hurried from the house in the grayish morning light. It was raining again, which didn't help my mood in the least. It seemed like gloomy times were to be expected by my fellow Germans during this glorious thing called war.

What had once been heralded as our saving grace, bringing our nation glory again, had taken a sharp turn in the opposite direction. I was thankful our family had been born to Aryan Aristocracy. None of us had a drop of the dreaded Jewish blood, which allowed us to survive being taken to the camps, unless the Gestapo discovered my other secret job.

My ancestry had saved me in another way. Marriage to an officer of the Reich was expected of women my age. Due to my family's influential connections in shipping, and the healthy donations to the cause, we were considered to be of great value. The arrogant men my boss was constantly introducing me to in the crazy hopes of getting me off his hands weren't even possible because of their lower standings in society.

The wind whipped under the edges of my skirt, causing a chill to run up and down my spine as I cast a last look at my home. Though I was technically safe from a forced marriage, or worse, there was a secret that if anyone found out would be the end of my freedom.

As I settled into my seat for the long ride across town, I thought back to when the changes to our country had begun back in early 1933.

The Jewish problem, as my employers had named it, was just the beginning of mass deportations and pogroms throughout the country.

Just having graduated from high school, I was allowed to be my father's secretary at his shipping company. While many of my friends were concerned with going to the university or getting married, I was learning the shipping trade from the top to the very bottom.

The Rosenblatts, our servants, had been with our family since my father's time. They weren't just servants, though. They were family to me. With the new laws, their future was looking dim. Foolishly, I'd conferred with my parents about what we were going to do about them.

"What are we going to do about Frau and Herr Rosenblatt?" I'd asked as I took a seat in the den with my parents after dinner one evening.

"There isn't anything to do, my dear. The Party has spoken, and for the present, we have to do what they want." The smell of my father's pipe filled the air as he spoke.

"Yes, my dear." Mama patted my arm in a consoling gesture. "We have always considered them family, but with the current climate, there really isn't any choice. We must let them go. I'm sure your father will give them a recommendation so that they can manage for a while until they find work among their own people."

That was the day I'd decided to work against my family and my country. I was going to become a traitor, and it was the first time I'd felt at peace.

Rain drops ran down the panes on the trolley car, cleaning the glass that had gone unwashed for months. While it was only a ten-minute walk, public transportation was one of the few safe ways for a young woman to travel without running into trouble. A few extra minutes' worth of detours were worth staying safe, especially when the trolley would drop me within a block of my job.

I could only wish the rain would wash away the trouble I now carried with me daily. The mask I'd so easily put on a few short years ago had become as much a part of me as I strove to be two completely different people. Dutiful, Aryan daughter of the Third Reich, and the traitor who rescued the very people I was supposed to despise and hate.

Even back then, I couldn't understand why the people who had always had a home with us should be expected to move out when they were getting into their golden years, when we should be taking care of them instead of throwing them out on the street.

My pleas for us to let them stay at our country home had gone unheeded, and I'd feared to mention it again as my brother, Ernst, had joined the Schutzstaffel, or the SS, as they came to be known as later. Our family wasn't going to do anything against the atrocities that were taking place, so I knew I was going to have to do something to balance out the horrors being done.

Shipping was what our family had always done, as was tradition, and I'd got them a special set of tickets to America, where they had siblings who'd immigrated there years before. That had been harder than I thought possible, due to the length of the passage, and the fact that I'd had to give the captain a substantial amount of money simply to make sure he would look out for them, and not alert authorities to their presence.

While we were a well-respected family, our ships and cargo were searched more thoroughly with each passing year. Anyone was willing to be an informant, especially if it meant they would be compensated for their help with money or a more prominent position.

When my father had been given the ultimatum to turn his ships over for the German cause, I thought I'd be out of a job. Our business was shipping, and without the ships, there wasn't a whole lot I could do at the office each day.

The commander had noticed my work when we'd transferred the ships and supplies. I was the one working out all the shipping details and keeping things running smoothly. When he asked if I would become his secretary, doing the same thing for the Third Reich in an official capacity, I'd had no choice but to say yes. My options were few and far between.

Now, ten years later, I'd become one of his most trusted assistants. If he had any idea of the type of covert operations, I ran under his very nose, he'd have me sent to one of the camps without hesitation.

The trolley slowed as it approached my stop, and I stood, shaking the traitorous thoughts from my mind as I prepared to disembark. While the Gestapo weren't mind readers, they were very good at ferreting out those who opposed them, and dying wasn't on my agenda for the day.

"Heil, Hitler." I saluted the guards on duty, who returned my greeting with the same tired response.

There had been so much passion behind the words in earlier years, but now we said the words by memory. Many had been arrested for not responding when greeted, and no one wanted to take a chance of being sent to the dreaded camps.

"Ah, Fraulein Thea. I am so glad you've arrived. We have several problems that need your special attention. The freight for our troops was loaded onto the wrong ship, and both captains are ready to riot at the delays," Captain Fuchs declared before I even got my coat off.

"Yes, sir." I pulled out the shipping manifest for both ships and checked off which of the items had been swapped. "Here is where the problem occurred. It's a simple fix. I'll call down and make the arrangements with the dock manager."

It hadn't been a mistake, but it was the only way to get needed supplies to some of the resistance fighting against our very own troops. When the miss-labeled supplies arrived, one of our networks would offer to take it off their hands, and no one would be the wiser.

The only thing that had gone wrong was that Captain Fuchs had been informed.

"Yes, those were the correct supplies, Johann. It was simply labeled wrong on the checklist. You're good to set sail." I glanced at a few of the more pressing items as I listened to his anger at being delayed. "I will make sure the commander knows that it's not your fault the ship was late. Although, it might help if you made up a little time and got there early, just in case there's a bonus waiting for you," I warned as I hung up the phone.

"You have such a way of solving problems. He'll be certain he isn't at fault, but will make sure he isn't late to receive a possible prize. He'll be too scared to ask about it, but hopefully enough to work harder to get there. Genius!" he exclaimed in delight. "Maybe it's you who deserves a raise instead."

I smiled flirtatiously at him. "Oh, I would never expect anything like that when I'm just performing my duties for the Reich."

He took his jacket and hat off the coat rack, draping them over his arm. "I've been called to a meeting with my superiors to find out if we can get even more supplies to our troops. They're not doing so well in the dratted Russian cold."

"Yes, sir. I'll handle anything that comes in, and if it's urgent, I'll put a memo on your desk if you haven't returned when I go to lunch."

I felt his gaze as I bent over to file the current papers in the cabinet.

"If only I was a younger man, you'd be having a different type of lunch break." He gave me a suggestive wink before closing the door gently behind him.

A sigh escaped my lips as the intense scrutiny left when he did. He was a harmless older man who'd been given his position based on his knowledge in the last world war. He was in his sixties, but I knew his wife, and he loved her dearly. It didn't hurt anything for him to look, especially when it offered me protection from others.

There were a few important matters I needed to attend to. I needed to order supplies so the old ones could be "thrown away" and given to those who needed them more, such as stamps for purchase orders and requisitions that would be used for many in need.

Before things had gotten bad, I'd purchased a sailboat for our country home, which had instead been delivered to the resistance for short trips to the Netherlands. After the invasion of the coast, it had become more difficult, but I knew the small boat still carried precious cargo over the seas to England.

Several of the friends I'd made over the years were doing the same type of work, and between us, we knew when it was the safest to send out a little boat through the dangerous waves.

The morning was spent fixing problems, both real and imagined, when the door opened to reveal my brother Ernst.

Though I was completely against everything he stood for, he was still my brother, and I was always glad to see he was alive and healthy.

"Ernst, you're home. Mother and Father will be so pleased to see you. Will you be here for long?" I gushed, hurrying from behind the desk to give him a warm embrace.

"That's a little more enthusiastic than I'd expected from you, Unruhestiftler." He laughed.

"Ernst, I'm not a troublemaker anymore. The only person I ever wanted to cause trouble for was you and your friends when you wouldn't let me play with you," I scoffed.

"Are you free for lunch? I've got a few things to discuss with you." While it sounded like an ordinary question, his tone implied there was more to it.

"Yes, of course. Captain Fuchs is at a meeting, and wasn't sure when he'd be back. Just let me leave him a note and lock up." I smiled, as if it was going to be the most exciting thing, but the pit of dread in my stomach didn't agree with my thoughts.

"I'll wait." He plopped into the empty seat across from my desk as he took in my office. "How are our parents? Did Father recover from his bout with the flu?"

"Um, yes. He's doing better. The doctor said when the weather gets warmer in the spring, it would go away entirely. For now, he's giving him medicine to get him through the winter."

We fell silent as I shuffled a few papers and placed them on the captain's desk.

"There, I think that should do it. Did you have a place in mind for lunch?" He'd been gone for a while, but I was certain he missed going to some of our favorite places.

He rose and held my coat out for me in an unusual bout of kindness. "I'm going to let you choose since you know which places still have good food with all the rationing.

Honestly, I'm just happy to have something that isn't cooked over an open fire."

While he sounded like my brother, there was something underneath that made me feel the need to be extra cautious with my responses. He exuded a sense of danger, which could probably be explained, but I preferred to err on the side of caution.

"A small place opened where Meyers used to be, and they've done wonders with the menu in light of the shortages." Many ignored the fact that some foods were rationed, or simply found ways to make it sound like we were doing it for our country. In reality, the city was starting to have problems feeding even the rich, while the poor went hungry all the time.

I tried to chat about normal, everyday things, in hopes it would make the weird feeling in my stomach go away.

As they seated us at one of the tables, Ernst turned the conversation to more serious topics.

"What do you think of your boss, Captain Fuchs?" His gaze searched my face, and I knew this was more than just an innocent question.

"He's very polite and protective of me, which I appreciate. Why do you ask?" I'd found that answering a question with one might get me more information.

"You don't feel he's too old to be doing his job properly?"

I shook my head. "No, he's not as young as some of the others doing their jobs in the war. Then again, he's not required to be out on the frontlines either. I don't think he's quite as capable as our father, but who is?"

"Hmm. I've just wondered if he might need to be replaced with someone new. That's part of the reason I'm in town. One of our heroes is being shown around, and I thought you might be a great guide for him. I can have him join me in my newest project to help a scientist with creating the perfect soldier, or he can have your boss's job." Crossing his arms, he gave me an appraising look. "In fact, I think I'm going to recommend him take over as your boss. Then, once he falls for you, we can have a wedding and some perfect little babies who can grow up to fight for the Fatherland." He laughed at the disgusted expression on my face.

Occasionally, I could be surprised by something, and the fact that my brother was trying to make me have some man's babies had certainly done just that.

"Seriously, Ernst, I'm not ready to get married, and I enjoy what I do for our Führer. Captain Fuchs wouldn't know what to do with retirement anyway," I protested playfully, hoping he was joking.

"I'll consider that. But don't be surprised if the German high command accepts my recommendation. It's time for Captain Fuchs to use his energy out on the front where his wisdom can be put to good use."

My hand flew to my mouth. "No, you wouldn't send him to the front, would you? He hasn't done anything that would justify such an action."

Normally, sending someone to the front meant they had really screwed up and were being punished.

"Don't worry, you'll like Wilhelm. He'll be here until we can find a more suitable replacement. I'd suggest if you don't want to be forced into a situation you might find repulsive, you provide your own appropriate man to take care of your situation," Ernst warned as he rose, gently kissing my cheek. His parting words left me sitting there in shock as he exited the café without eating.

His brotherly affection had been to get a reaction, planning to enact this horrible disgrace on me. I was nothing but a way to further his career. A bargaining chip to gain a promotion.

There had to be some way out of this, but I was going to have to work hard and fast to figure out something to get around becoming a breeder for some SS soldier. My poor boss was going to be harder to save, and he would go to the front without a fight because he was doing it for his country. I might not be able to convince him to leave, even if it meant living longer.

The food I'd ordered arrived, but any appetite I'd had was gone. Instead, I paid for the meal and left. For all I knew, my brother was having me watched, and I'd need to be careful until he returned to whatever hole he'd crawled out of.

CHAPTER FIVE

—·—

THEA

The office was empty when I arrived, and I hurried to lock the door behind me. I still had some time from my lunch break, and this room was one of the few places I could think without prying eyes.

I sank into my chair and laid my head down on the desk.

It wasn't as if I didn't want to find a husband, but the idea of marrying a Nazi was the very definition of dying a horrible death to me. Any man with a moral fiber was already working for the resistance, and I couldn't be seen associating with them, or they'd be sent to one of the camps.

If by some chance there was a man out there I didn't loathe, it would be a miracle.

Then there was the whole problem of trying to keep Captain Fuchs from being sent to the Russian front. The cold would be horrible for his arthritis, and he wouldn't last a week with the younger men.

I could try to convince him to leave before getting on the train, or find a way to go somewhere else where he wouldn't die. Not everyone could be saved, but I hated that someone I knew was being sent to his death for no reason.

A tentative knock on the door brought my head up. Only someone with authority or a sense of urgency would expect to find anyone in the offices during lunch.

Standing quickly, I glanced in the mirror to make sure no signs of my mental anguish were visible.

I flicked the lock and opened the door to find a tall blond man standing in front of me.

"May I help you?" I inquired with a raised brow.

"Uh, I hope so." He glanced down at a paper in his hand. "This is the office of the shipping master, isn't it?"

I shook my head and stepped back, holding the door open. "Yes. Please, come in."

Hesitantly, he entered and stood awkwardly as I closed the door and rounded my desk.

Plastering a smile on my face, I motioned to the chair for him to take a seat. "You're in the right spot. What is it you need help with?" My voice was back to pleasant as I stepped easily into my role as the secretary of shipping.

He shrugged, seeming uncertain. "Major Weber told me to report here for my assignment. I'm not sure exactly what I'm supposed to do, as I know nothing about shipping."

My hand flew to my mouth when I realized he was the man my brother wanted me to sleep with. Not that this was as abhorrent of an idea as it had been only moments ago, as I took in his strength and regal bearing.

Heat rose in my cheeks. "Oh, my. I–I'm so sorry, sir," I stammered. "I had no idea who you were. I wasn't informed that Captain Fuchs wouldn't be returning today."

In his haste to stand, he dropped his hat to the floor. "It's completely my fault. I thought you'd been told of the changes. Considering I only found out I wouldn't be returning to the France this morning, it's not surprising."

"Well, let me give you a tour. What should I call you?" I questioned, holding out my hand for his hat that he'd retrieved from the floor.

He held out his hand. "Captain Gradl von Boden, Fräulein?"

"Fräulein Weber. I'm Major Weber's sister."

I took his outstretched hand in mine, but instead of shaking it, he brought it to his lips and kissed my knuckles.

"Um, right this way." I took my hand back in surprise. It had been a while since a gentleman had greeted me in such a way.

"So, shipping is vital to our troops. This will be your office, and you'll be coordinating with merchants to provide food, uniforms, ammunition, and anything else they tell us to ship," I provided as he glanced around the small office. "If you don't mind me asking, how did you get recommended for this position, Captain Gradl von Boden?"

If he was going to be my new boss, I would need to know something about him. Just because my brother had gotten him the job, didn't mean he wasn't a horrible person hiding behind a handsome face.

"Please, there's no need to stand on formality if we're going to be working together, unless it would make you uncomfortable. You may call me Wilhelm."

"How about we compromise on Captain Wilhelm? I'd hate to get into trouble for not treating an officer with the proper respect he deserves." I walked toward the door. "I'll let you look through things, and if you have any questions, feel free to ask me."

"I don't deserve any respect," he mumbled as I pulled the door closed behind me.

He hadn't answered my question, but I was sure all of this was a bit overwhelming for him.

For the rest of the afternoon, I answered the phone and took care of the most pressing issues that couldn't wait.

A little before four, he finally stuck his head out of his office.

"Fräulein Weber, I'm not sure how anything got done in here. Most of the papers don't even make sense, and there isn't any sense of order as to what goes out and what comes in." He held a handful of papers in one hand, while running the other through his well-combed hair.

There was much to say at this point, since Captain Fuchs had been sent away. It wasn't like there was a worse punishment than being sent to the Russian front.

"May I be frank with you, sir?"

"Yes, please."

"Captain Fuchs kept mostly to himself, and accompanied me to the shipping docks for protection when I needed to take care of a problem. Otherwise, he spoke mostly with merchants and brought me the lists, which I took care of making sure products went on the correct ships and destinations the Wehrmacht officers gave us."

"So, you mean to tell me, you know sensitive information about our troops and their locations?" His tone had changed from friendly to accusatory.

"Well, yes, sir, it's part of my job. If we sent coats to the southern part of France instead of the Russian border, our troops would be in a real mess," I hurried to assure him.

"I don't want to speak ill of your previous boss, but honestly, I'm not sure you're supposed to have that kind of information. I guess if the Gestapo haven't made any inquiries or issued any concerns, then it must not be much of a problem. Still, once I've come to understand how this office works, we'll revisit this issue." His tone had softened a little at my alarmed expression.

"Yes, sir," I murmured through dry lips. If he had any idea how close he'd come to finding out the truth...

"Do you have much more to finish up with today?"

"No, sir," I answered, keeping it short.

"Very well. Let's lock up, and we can start fresh in the morning." He closed Captain Fuchs's office door behind him before heading to the coat rack. "Do you have any recommendations on where to get some food in this area?"

While my stomach rolled at the thought of him uncovering some of my actions, I did the only thing that would be considered appropriate for someone in his position.

"Would you like to come to dinner at my parent's home? They would be thrilled to meet my new boss, and I'd never hear the end of it if I let you run off to find something on your own here in the city," I offered, drumming up a smile.

The best way to keep him from questioning things in the office might be for him to get to know me better. Even though my brother might not have my best interests in mind, he might have come up with the only solution to my problems.

"I couldn't impose on you like that. It wouldn't be right," he protested as I locked up the office.

"No, it wouldn't be an imposition. Ration cards haven't stopped my parents' staff from putting out a decent meal. It's one of the few perks of living with them during the war."

"All right, then. I won't say no a second time to the offer of a home cooked meal. I've been with my unit for a long time, and real food is something I was certain I'd only imagined existed while out there."

"Then, I insist. But you have to tell me what it was like out there. I've heard stories of the horrors from enemy artillery and tanks."

"I'll tell you what I can, but most of it wouldn't be appropriate to repeat in a lady's company." He offered his arm to me, which I accepted almost eagerly.

It had been a while since I'd been on a date, as more of our soldiers were gone, and I never knew who I might be going out with. So, being escorted by a handsome German man might not be as horrible as I'd originally thought.

● ● ● ● ● ● ● ● ● ● ●

My parents were ecstatic that I'd brought home an officer. It had been months since we'd had company, and they quickly pounced on him with questions.

"Wilhelm, are the French as trying as the papers say they are?" my father inquired, unconcerned with using the captain's first name and not his rank.

"Well, sir, I honestly didn't see much of the French in the army's fortified areas. We were on the borders, making sure nothing tried to land and attack us. It was intense last year, but since we've claimed the French territory, there has been very little fighting in the French cities," he answered slowly, trying to eat in a dignified manner while fielding the barrage directed at him.

The maid had just begun to serve dessert when the front door opened, and my brother strode in, looking as if he was the ruler of the world.

"Ernst, my son, we didn't know you were in town. Come, join us. You're just in time for dessert. Have you met Wilhelm Gradl von Boden?" my mother gushed as she hurried to give him a hug.

He smiled over at me as he brushed off her attempt at affection.

"Yes, Mother. I'm the one who recommended him to take over as Thea's boss. Someone needs to keep an eye on her, and it might as well be a trustworthy officer of the Reich." His blatant suggestion was followed up with a wink in my direction.

"Ms. Weber was of tremendous help today. I'm sure I'll figure out where everything goes in no time at all," Wilhelm kindly acknowledged.

"Anything for our troops." I smiled at him, completely ignoring my brother. Now that he'd arrived, I wouldn't be able to sneak out and find a way to get Captain Fuchs smuggled to safety.

"It's so nice to be home and see that nothing has really changed." Ernst didn't even glance at the maid as she brought out an extra dessert for him.

"A few things have changed, but we've tried so hard to keep our spirits up while remembering those of you who are on the frontlines," Father assured Ernst. "If only I was young enough to be of more help."

I listened to the conversation flowing around me and realized for the first time that my parents were scared of their own son. Each sentence spoken was worded so carefully and filled with glowing praise for the Führer.

When Father asked, "Would you gentlemen care to join me for a cigar?" I waited with bated breath to see how much longer I was going to be required to keep up my false pleasantness.

Ernst slung an arm over Wilhelm's shoulders. "Certainly. We have time for that now, don't we, Wilhelm?"

"Yes, sir. But then, I must return to my hotel room so I'll be well-rested for tomorrow."

"It's all work and no play with you, Wilhelm. I'll have to issue it an order for you to have fun while you're here. Once you get things situated, I'm going to take you for a drive out into the countryside next week."

He raised an eyebrow as I edged away toward my room. When the door was closed, I turned and fled, unsure if I should try to leave or wait and see what my brother had in store for the rest of the evening.

The shrill sound of a phone rang loudly through the house before my brother came racing out of the door he'd just closed.

"Thank you for a lovely evening, sir," Wilhelm commented as I paused on the stair landing. "I really must return to my hotel. I'm not used to all this normal behavior after months on the battlefield. Please, give your wife my apologies."

He left, but not before glancing up the stairs to where I stood.

"I'll see you tomorrow." Tipping his head in my direction, he fled through the door my brother had rushed out of moments before.

Maybe he wouldn't be such a bad fellow after all if he didn't want to be around my brother any more than I did. We could help each other without raising a fuss.

• • • ● ● • ● ● • • •

The front door slamming shut woke me from a sound sleep. Ernst must have come home.

Other doors were opened and shut until the house finally fell silent once more. With all the changes of wartime, I'd taken to locking my door years ago, but it wouldn't keep out someone who was persistent.

My brother might not respect many things, but I didn't fear him trying to do something horrible to me. Yet, if I didn't take his suggestions to heart, he would want to know what I was hiding. I had to protect the innocent at all costs.

PART 2

1943-1944

CHAPTER SIX

CAMERON

SOMEWHERE IN AFRICA

There was sand everywhere. It was in my ass, the food, the water, and in my lungs.

When someone had written that war was hell, I'm not sure that they understood the meaning of the word. It was absolutely an understatement if I'd ever heard one.

I'd arrived on the scene with my platoon almost two years ago, bright-eyed and ready to beat the Nazis back to Germany, where they belonged.

How wrong I had been, I thought as I ducked down to avoid the spray of debris from one of the tanks constantly shooting in our direction.

They couldn't move from the line where they'd parked almost a year ago because of our mines and constant barrage anti-tank guns pinning them down. It had been a stand-off, but we'd been ordered to hold this position no matter what.

We couldn't let the tanks come past the outer boundaries or we'd lose the town just a few miles out of range. It was the center for our headquarters, but it also doubled as the main village that supplied received food from the surrounding area.

I hated war; it was horrible. What had at first seemed to be so glamourous was now my worst nightmare. The first battle had been a learning experience, having to watch as men were blown up. Even Pope had quit making jokes those first few days until he'd gotten used to the gore and realities of war.

"What do you think? Will they be able to hit that new rock we put on the hill last night with a bullseye painted on it?"

Even with all the people I'd met over my time out here in the desert, Pope still held the record for the dumbest ideas that might get you killed while having fun.

"Trade you a pack of cigs if it turns out you're right," he challenged.

Spitting in my hand, I held it out to seal the deal. "They only got another three hours until the shift is over to make it."

"Eh, they can't miss it. It's right there calling to them." He popped his head over the barricade to look at it. "Nah. They're not even coming close to it."

Something was happening that distracted me from Pope's words.

A truck had pulled up to the command center with what appeared to be a general with his assistant. It was the woman from the boat that had sunk.

She held her hand up to block out the bright sunshine. Her brown hair was pinned up, but it wasn't keeping the sand from blowing into it while she tried to remain dignified.

We got dignitaries who came through on a regular basis, but most of the time, we didn't actually interact with them. This time was different, though. I was going to make sure I found out who she was.

"I'll be back." I jumped up, brushing at my uniform to make it look a bit more presentable. It was a losing battle, obviously, but I at least wanted to try.

"Where are you..." He followed me as I walked toward the jeep. "Deserting me in the desert for a chick? Figures."

They were talking amongst themselves, so I hung back just enough that I couldn't hear anything I wasn't supposed to, but where I could introduce myself when the opportunity presented itself.

Sergeant Pittman blocked my path with his body. "May I help you, Private O'Malley?"

"Yes, sir. I have a date with the universe when they're finished talking to the major." I stood at attention, hoping he wouldn't stop me, because I'd just have to find another way to meet her.

He glanced behind us to where they were still deep in conversation. "She is a looker, but I think you're way out of your league. Can't hurt for you to try, I guess."

"Thank you, sir." Relief filled me as he returned my salute and moved aside.

He patted me on the back as I passed by. "Good luck."

They were just breaking up as I approached, so I slid my helmet off and ran a nervous hand through my hair.

"Um, hi." I cleared my throat, as it came out more of a croak than words that made sense.

"Hello." She gave me a smile that shined brighter than the midday sun.

"I'm Private Cameron O'Malley, at your service." I gave her a salute due to the bars that were on her uniform.

"Thank you, Private O'Malley, but the general has taken care of all our arrangements for our stay here." She returned my salute and started to turn away.

"Ma'am, I don't mean to be impolite, but I was there the day you were rescued from that battleship. It was a good thing you did that day. I've just felt the need to meet you."

Her sigh told me that this wasn't the first time that this had happened to her.

"Look, Cameron, I'm going to be frank with you. I lost my fiancé during the attack on Pearl Harbor. I'm not really looking for a relationship of any kind. As WACs, we're not really supposed to engage in fraternization of that type with the troops. I'm really sorry." She was almost back to the jeep when I caught her attention.

"Could I please have your name so I can write to you?" I pleaded. "I lost a brother at Pearl Harbor, and it would be nice to have someone to talk to who understands. If not, I completely understand."

When she didn't respond, I put my hat back in place, preparing to go back to the barricade.

"It's Officer Irene Fitzgerald, care of General Eisenhower's attaché," she called out to me.

With a grin, I gave her a wave of thanks. "I'll get it sent off to you. Thank you."

The bounce in my step couldn't be replaced by anything else in the world at that moment. She'd given me her name, and I was going to make the most of that little crack in the door.

Another round from the tanks started, and Pope let out a loud "Whoop!" as the Axis finally hit the bullseye on the rock.

I was never going to hear the end of this, but right now, I didn't even care that I owed him a pack of cigs.

• • • ● ● ● ● ● • •

Letter to Irene from Cameron

Officer Fitzgerald,

I can't express the joy you gave me when you told me your name today. It's been a long time since I had someone to talk to who wasn't one of the men in my unit.

We've all seen more than we would like to, and know that war is a harsh reality where we could be dead in just a few seconds.

While I can understand your need for only a friendship, I'll be honest, as I can only hope that one day you might be able to see me in a different light.

My family is from the south of Montana, and I so miss the large open spaces filled with trees and grass. The fresh air of back home is so different from the heat that never seems to die here where I'm stationed.

Can you believe the amount of sand here in this retched place? I'm sure you have a certain amount of comfort from the discomforts on the battlefield, being one of his assistants and all, and for that, I envy you.

Anyway, this is getting long for a first letter, so I'll just wait and see what kind of questions you have for me.

Thanks for the chance to be your friend,

Cameron.

Response to Cameron from Irene

Cameron,

Hey there! You can just call me Irene. It feels a little strange to have you calling me by my official title, when honestly, we are pretty much the same. I have no real authority and just translate for my boss. Since I speak French, he brought me along on his trip to meet you.

I've been in mourning for a long time, and it was nice to meet someone who took me at face value. Most of the guys I've met haven't been concerned with anything but a quick roll in the hay. (I don't mean to be vulgar, but I do have a job in the army.)

Let's take things slow and see where we're both at at the end of the war. And yes, I do hate the sand. I'm used to a much different environment, and being on the actual field of battle is not what I expected. That one dunk in the ocean was more than enough of a brush with death than I ever want to have again.

I'm from Washington D.C., and my mom and dad are both are survivors of the last Great War. When Pearl Harbor happened, the only way I could cope with my grief was to do something productive. I thought that by joining what was then called the WAACs, I could free up someone who could fight instead of doing paperwork.

Now that so many have taken our joining with the military in the wrong way, all the WACs need to take great care that they aren't caught in any compromising positions. We must be above reproach, and to be the best soldiers we can be.

Anyway, I'd love to get to know you better, and I look forward to our next letter.

Irene.

• • • ● ● • ● ● • •

As the months went by, her letters were the only things I found myself looking forward to each day. Some days, or weeks, there would be no response, but that was because the mail couldn't make it through as easily with every other ship being fired on by the Germans.

Pope teased me unmercifully, but I knew I needed to keep this part of my world to myself. Occasionally, I would tell him a small thing I'd learned, but mostly I'd hurry to respond so that the letter could go out the same day.

Months of sand and heat had made our brains go soft. We couldn't even make headway against the armies that were trying to besiege us. They'd changed things up and attacked the village, so we'd had to move back. Then, a week later, we were told to evacuate to a new area where we were able to push them back and win a decisive battle.

There were no letters for almost three weeks, and I'd begun to despair, thinking she no longer wanted to correspond with me. While I knew it might take time to get the mail to where we were, even as we were killing other men and trying to gain a foothold in North Africa, I still craved her words. It was like a little bit of home in the midst of battle.

Bullets whizzed by my head as I tried to find a position with enough cover to be out of harm's way and return fire.

Anderson fell into place beside me, breathing heavily from the large expanse of terrain we'd just run across.

"Are they ever going to run out of ammo?"

"Nope," I returned. "They're planning to wipe us all out. It's part of their master plan, remember?"

"Can one of us gain enough of a position where we can knock out that sharpshooter's nest?" Anderson looked at Booth in the little nook beside us.

"I heard that!" he hollered. "I'm going for it. Make sure I have enough cover."

Unable to charge through the bullets quietly, he gave a war-cry as he jumped into their nest, leaving a handful of grenades behind as he raced behind one of the sand dunes.

I shook my head at his lack of care. "Seriously, you'd think he'd have learned to be more cautious."

He grinned in anticipation. "Then we wouldn't be moving forward at the same pace so the others can follow us into their main camp. We might actually have a partial win today."

"I'll settle for a bed and a hot meal."

"You sure don't have big goals, do you? We'd better get over there, or Booth's going to have all the fun."

"Yep." I moved my weary body over the top of the crevice, hoping there was a bed in my future.

Chapter Seven

Irene

"Hey!" Clara called out to me as I headed out to lunch. "You've got another one of those letters from that guy."

A smile broke out on my face as I hurried to catch up with her. "Thanks. It's been a while since I've gotten one from him. They've had some big battles and moving around a lot, so it's been hard to get the mail through."

She passed me the envelope, with sand still clinging to it.

"You really like him, don't you?"

"I didn't at first, but he's grown on me. For one thing, he's not here in my face, pressuring me to get involved, and it's been nice to have someone to tell things to who isn't with me all the time," I admitted as I fell into step beside her.

She got this dreamy look on her face. "That's so wonderful. I'd love to find one guy who wasn't shipping out in a few days. I need my man to be nearby, and not that close to the death and dying in a war."

"Makes sense, but I'm not ready to be in a relationship," I stated firmly, opening the door to the mess hall.

"Right. And what do you call this long-distance flirtation that makes you smile when you get the newest missive?" she challenged.

"Well, I guess I'm just glad he's alive. If we make it through this war, then I'll consider seeing if we have something that can make it through regular, everyday life. Most of the time, these guys sound really good, but in reality, they're just normal guys looking for the next girl who will give them what they want."

"Wow. You are so cynical. I know you lost your fiancé, but that wasn't his fault. Not all guys are that bad, and there are even a few good ones if you'll just give them a chance." Her shocked expression clued me in that maybe I was being a little too hard on the opposite sex when I wasn't working.

"I'll try to look at it with an open mind. I hadn't realized I was so transparent about my distaste for the players with girlfriends in the States, but try to hook up with these unsuspecting English girls." I grimaced at the thought of how many times I'd seen some doughboy writing a letter home, only to be out with a new girl later that afternoon.

"True, but you can't believe the majority of the men here are doing that." She took her tray and searched for a place to sit. "Really, you should start dating and get your feet wet again. Then, when you do get a chance to go out with Cameron, it won't be a disaster because you're so rusty."

"At least I know what you think. Please, don't hold back." I grinned so she wouldn't take it personally.

"On to other news besides your very sad and lacking love life. Did you hear they've brought in a group of women from the States to help clear the backlog of letters that aren't being delivered?"

"I hadn't heard that, but I'm not surprised. We simply don't have the manpower to take care of that kind of thing. Who are they bringing over for it? More WACs?" I took a bite of the carrot dish and instantly wished for home.

"Um, I think they're WACs, but they're part of a special division of the Central Postal Directory Battalion. Sounds all official for just sorting the mail, huh?" Clara chuckled.

Jewell Payne from one of the other WAC units spoke up from the table next to us. "Actually, they call themselves the Six Triple Eights, and from what I understand, they're going to clear that warehouse out of the mail backlog."

Frowning, I held up Cameron's letter. "I'm not sure I understand why we'd need an entire battalion to do that. I got my mail just today, and it's only a week old."

Jewell leaned closer to our table. "There's mail and packages that have been in this warehouse for the past two years. The number of letters going back and forth just weren't the priority, but when the general learned about it, he took action."

"The Postal Battalion is almost as important in the keeping up of moral for our men as the nurses are in helping them recover from their wounds. Wounds on the soul are much worse than those inflicted by the enemy. We have to bring our men some joy, happiness, and a little piece of home," she quoted the general with ease. "I've been working on their arrival and making sure they have quarters to stay in."

"My gracious, I had no idea. I guess I've been taking the fact that my letters get delivered so quickly for granted." I couldn't believe there was mail that hadn't made it to the troops for almost two years.

"Yes," Clara twittered. "There are almost a thousand of them, correct?"

"Yep," Jewell whispered quietly. "This is a special division made up of women of color."

"Why would that be a bad thing?" I queried, not sure I understood what she was implying.

"Well, it's just highly unusual for women of color to be allowed to come overseas."

"So you're telling me they went through the same training we did, want to help their country, and that's unusual because of their skin color? I think it's insane that would even be an issue." I'd had about all the food and prejudice I could stomach for my meal. I stood up and nodded politely before I said more that might get us all into trouble.

A messenger caught up to me as I exited the building, still angry over Jewell's preconception regarding fellow officers. "Officer Fitzgerald, you've been requested in the general's headquarters to help with a few translations."

"Of course," I acknowledged, changing course.

When I arrived at the main headquarters, it was a buzz with something unusual.

"What's going on?" I asked the harried looking operator sitting at the switchboard.

"They've got news of a massive series of explosions the underground has managed to pull off. The Germans are pissed, and the French are ready to party, but that would only get them arrested." She nodded at the door to the conference room. "They want you in there."

"Got it." With a deep breath, I opened the door and hurried inside.

"There you are," the general's aide, Vance Collins, greeted as he pulled me aside. "We've gotten some reports of things that are happening in France today, but there are few that need to be translated before they can be decoded."

"Yes, sir." I took the brief and began to read through it for the first time. It was always better to get an understanding of the missive before I tried to translate it word by word.

A headache was forming after the first few documents were finished and in the hands of the decoders. It was time for me to take a small break and stretch my legs.

I'd forgotten all about Cameron's letter hidden in my pocket, but there wasn't time for me to take a peek at what he'd written, because the messages I was working on were much more important.

Thankfully, the loo—as the Brits insisted on calling them—didn't have a line, and I was able to take care of business before hurrying behind the building where all the girls managed to grab a smoke when they could.

Clara was standing there, and from the looks of her frazzled hair, she had been just as busy as I had been.

I took the pack out of my pocket and held one up. "Got a light?" No matter how much I might disagree with her views, I was still her friend, and those were few and far between out here in the mostly boys' club.

"Yes." As she flicked the lighter, I brought the cigarette to my lips.

Inhaling, I leaned against the back wall. "Ah, that was what I needed to help clear my head."

We weren't really supposed to smoke, as it wasn't appropriate, according to Director Hobby, but she wasn't here, and it was one of the few things that could help release the stress and frustration.

"They got you busy translating?"

"Uh-huh. I've got hours more to go, and my eyes feel like they're starting to bleed." I rubbed at them, wishing I hadn't worn mascara.

Clara lit another cigarette, taking advantage of her small moment of freedom. "Girl, my ears are starting to ring because of the constant buzzing and answering the boards out there.".

"I feel your pain." I dropped my still smoking butt into the small can that had been placed for our use. "Well, I've got to get back to it. Life and death don't take breaks."

Clara stuck her tongue out at me, but took a long drag from her smoke and quickly put it out, knowing I was right.

The air had felt good, but it wasn't until I was back inside the shit really hit the fan.

"The Germans are gaining ground in Russia at a place called Demyansk," Collins read from a telegram handed to him. "Sir, if the Russians lose, then it's going to cause problems with Mr. Stalin."

I didn't speak Russian, but a few of the other translators did, and the room was suddenly filled with a mix of English and Russian, as if what had been happening in France was no longer important.

"Can we get an accurate count of the losses there?" General Eisenhower questioned the group.

"As accurate as any other information we get from Mother Russia." Someone in the room chuckled. "It would be better if they just got married, then sent armies to fight with each other and leave the rest of the world in peace."

It was a common joke around the Allied command that Father Germany and Mother Russia were a match made in heaven. Honestly, the only reason we hadn't all been overrun was that they didn't like each other, and Russia was willing to join us in the fight to help get rid of Hitler.

Unwilling to worry about it at present, I picked up the messages where I'd left off. They weren't going to translate themselves, and they were still important, just not as urgent at the moment.

• • • ● ● • ● ● • •

Twenty-four hours later, I had finished translating all the messages, slept for about five hours, and had been asked to return to headquarters for a briefing.

"Do we know what's happening?" I whispered to Clara as I inhaled the coffee and roll I'd been able to snatch up before the meeting started.

She leaned in close and informed me, "There are rumors of a defector who might have information for us. No one knows where they're from or who it is."

"May I have your attention, please?" Collins tapped the podium. "It has come to our attention that the enemy is using a new type of weapon. We are unsure of the capabilities of this weapon, and at the moment, only have the say so of a German woman, but it appears she may have urgent information for us."

"Is that what caused the Germans to win yesterday at Demyansk?" a lieutenant questioned from the back of the room.

"Right now, we don't know. There are rumors of some sort of super soldiers, or super troopers, as I've been told. It's not known if these were used against the Russian forces yet. They'd been fighting in or near the area of Demyansk for several months, and may have simply determined they were going to charge that area no matter the cost. We just don't have all the information at present," Collins explained in a rush.

"Will the person be able to give us more information when they arrive? Are we sending someone to Russia to get more on these storm troopers?" Clara asked from beside me.

"No, we can't send anyone to Russia. Right now, we simply have to rely on information that's passed to us by our Allies." He waved off the groans that erupted at his response. "I know it's not very reliable, but it's all we have at the moment. When we find out what these storm troopers are made of, or how they've engineered them, then we'll update everyone. They have to have a weakness."

"Do we think they're humans, and not some kind of robot?" someone from the other side of the room hollered without raising their hand.

"Seriously?" Collins responded with exasperation. "This is not some venture into the world of make believe. These guys wiped out an entire group of Russian soldiers. While I know you don't think much of our Allied counterparts, they are made of sterner stuff, and wouldn't go down easy in a fight. Let's give them a little credit for knowing what was trying to kill them. So, if there aren't any other real questions, then I'll be going back to helping us save lives." He scanned the room and left, dismissing us.

"Where do you think he goes when he's trying not to be disturbed?" Clara wondered. "He's really cute when he's riled up."

I could feel my eyes rolling at the comment. "Really? So now you want to chase after him because he's cute when he's mad? What kind of relationship would that be?"

My words must have registered, because she accused, "Why do you always have to do that?"

"What? I'm not doing anything except pointing out how exhausting it would be."

"You ruin everything. I can't try to date him now because you've made him seem like a monster. We could have been happy together. What about yesterday, huh? You just had to point out that we weren't being fair to all those women because they were colored."

"Um, Clara, I hate to be the bearer of bad news, but people shouldn't be judged on their skin tone or what country they're from. Just like Collins couldn't, or shouldn't be, expected to be mad just so you can find him cute. Quit making judgements on the outside and decide people's worth based on what's on the inside of their hearts," I huffed.

Jewell had approached without me realizing it.

"I'm glad to hear you feel that way. You're about to have a new set of roommates. Clara, you're reassigned to bunkhouse E. Please, go and collect your things. Irene, if you'll follow me, I'll introduce you to your new charge."

She took off at a brisk pace, not stopping until we arrived at the cafeteria building.

A scared looking blonde was huddled over two small children, as if she could save them from being hurt with her rail thin body.

"Irene, this is Thea Boden. You'll be helping her get acclimated to her quarters, and finding someone who can manage the children while she's working." Jewell smiled, as if I was being punished, but little did she know, I didn't mind at all.

"Sure. I'd be happy to." It made sense, because Clara and I's room was the largest in the C dorm.

"She speaks German, French, Russian, and English, though that's a little spotty. I'm sure it will get better as she has the chance to practice more. Anyway, I'll leave the two of you to get acquainted. Irene will take care of any problems that may come up." She paused before handing me a certificate of authority. "Only use this if it's absolutely necessary."

"Um, is it okay if I let the children eat before we go somewhere else?" Thea asked quietly.

"Of course." I gave her, the girl, and the boy a wide smile. "In fact, I haven't had a chance to eat myself and would love to join you."

Her tired eyes held a look of gratitude, but she simply nodded and began cutting up the vegetables into small bites.

When I returned, both the boy and girl were slowly picking at the food as if it couldn't be real.

"So, how did you come to be here, Mrs. Boden?" I took a bite, so happy I'd gotten a chance to eat more than that roll from earlier.

She ducked her head instinctively. "Well, it's Gradl von Boden, actually, but they said people might persecute us if they knew we were Germans."

"I'm sorry about that, but they are correct. It's best they assume you're just a refuge instead of a former German worker. We won't discuss that anymore so that you stay safe," I assured her, knowing exactly why Jewell had put this poor woman and her children in my room.

"The general said I was to rest, and that he would meet with me tomorrow." She cast a worried look around the room at all of the officers who were eating.

"He's a very nice man. Once we get you settled and get some rest where you don't have to watch over your shoulder, I'm sure things will start to look up a little bit." From the bags under her eyes, it appeared she hadn't slept in days.

"It's been a long journey, and with the baby only a month away from being born, it'll be nice to have somewhere to stay."

"Oh my gracious, I didn't realize." I wasn't sure how that was going to change things, but we needed to get her food and rest on a regular basis. "If you think the children are ready, we can get you settled in for some proper sleep."

The little ones had cleaned their plates, but didn't ask for seconds. In fact, for two small children, they had been extremely quiet during their meal.

"How old are they?" I asked, as Thea tried to pick them both up. Holding out my arms, the little girl came into them willingly.

"Will is three, and Hope's one." Thea hefted his thin body onto her hip as if he weighed nothing.

"They're such good kids." Hope had snuggled into my arms, putting her thumb into her mouth. "Do they understand English?"

"Yes. I've been using both German and English with them since birth. I was afraid this day might come and wanted them to be able to communicate if anything happened to me." She seemed resigned to the idea she could at some point be separated from them.

I guess during wartime; it was a real possibility. I wouldn't want to be a mother faced with those kinds of decisions. Then again, it wasn't like you could choose to be a mom or not; the universe made those choices for most of us.

It wasn't a very long walk, but I was afraid she would soon collapse.

"Here we are." I tried to keep my voice upbeat and cheerful so I didn't scare the children. "Beds, and a door that locks so you won't be disturbed."

Thea surveyed the room and moved toward the empty bed where Clara had removed her things from. Jewell had provided sheets and blankets for them all, and I sat Hope on my bed so I could set them up quickly.

"While you sleep, I'll go see about getting some clothes, toys, and a few things the children might need during your stay."

I straightened after tucking in a corner of the bed to find her wiping her eyes.

"Thank you. You are so kind." Her voice shook a bit as she laid Will on the bed.

"Do they need new nappies?" I didn't have anything that would remotely work for that sort of thing.

"No. He'll tell us when he needs to go, and I changed Hope just before we ate. I have one more clean set in my bag." I brought her over to the bed and removed her little shoes as she stared up at me with big eyes.

Thea sat at the foot, but made no move to lay down with them.

"Thea, would you feel more comfortable if I left?" I wasn't sure if she would be able to rest, considering she hadn't had much of it in the past few weeks.

Her mouth held the hint of a smile. "I'll wait until I'm sure they're out. This is the first time in months I've felt safe enough to sleep." "Well, I have a key, so I'll lock it and use mine when I have all the things you'll need over the next few days. Get some rest." I felt the need to get away before I burst into tears at the hopelessness of her situation.

My last view was of her laying down. If I'd only had an inkling of what she was thinking, it would've made my blood run cold at the terrors she'd been through the past few years.

CHAPTER EIGHT

THEA

It had all happened really fast. Four years of romance and happiness in the middle of a horrible war that was going to change the course of my life forever. Now I was lying in the headquarters for the Allied forces, and they desperately needed the information I was bringing them.

Thinking back to when my brother Ernst had suggested I fall in love with Wilhelm, I hadn't realized how easy it would be to do just that.

He was everything all the other men in my life hadn't been: honest, noble, and willing to do anything to make me happy.

We'd gotten married, and due to the war, had accepted a small apartment as a wedding gift from the army.

I'd been determined to continue working, even though I'd become pregnant within weeks of our consummation. I'd hid it well into my seventh month.

Since Wilhelm was my boss, as well as my husband, he was able to make sure I could stay in the office, out of sight, while he visited the docks and took care of any problems that occurred.

I had wanted to be completely honest with him, but since he was an honorable German, I knew I couldn't tell him about my work with the resistance. Not only would he not understand, but there was the danger that he'd feel it was his duty to inform the high command, ensuring I was sent to Dachau after the baby was born.

My activities had taken on a new danger because I couldn't be caught, or I would be dooming my child to death. Wilhelm would be blamed, and there would be nothing I could do to keep my family safe.

Ernst visited quite often after I married Wilhelm, and the two had developed an uneasy friendship. After one of their trips to the countryside, I'd tried to talk to him about his unsettled mood.

"Dearest, what's bothering you so much? I had hoped a drive in the fresh air would help to clear your head." I curled up next to him on our small sofa, willing him to feel better.

He sighed loudly. "I'm not sure I can tell you, as it's supposed to be a secret, but it's so horrible, I don't want to believe it."

This was serious, I thought, and sat up to hear what he was going to say.

"You can't tell anyone about this. Promise me?" he pleaded.

"I promise." I wanted to be a kid again and cross my fingers behind my back, but instead, I sat there while he explained the terrifying plans that were being made.

"They're going to take soldiers, some of our best and brightest, as well as a few of our worst, and inject them with this serum to see if it compelled them to... well, in Dr. Rudi's words, 'Storm the gates. Our Storm Troopers.' He'd just laughed at the idea." Wilhelm shuddered. "Your brother thinks this is the most wonderful thing ever, and is trying to find enough recruits so that when it's approved by the German High Command, they'll be ready to implement it."

"Dearest, what does the serum do to these soldiers to make them so strong?" I questioned, not fully understanding the danger this experiment would bring to the world.

"Remember those dinners he was always taking me to where we discussed the value of life versus the expanding of our weapons? I thought we were talking about real weapons, not men who had been turned into weapons. I've pleaded with them, giving the excuse that science wasn't really my thing, but Ernst took me to see a demonstration today. They allowed prisoners to be eaten by these animal-like humans. Not really human anymore, because they couldn't eat people in that manner if they were still human. I'm not sure what he did to them, but they appeared dead. When live people were brought out into this arena, these things attacked them. No questions, no issues. Just took off and tore into them."

"Oh, no. What's stopping them from doing that to our army?" I wasn't sure I was understanding what exactly he was saying.

"Nothing. Absolutely nothing." He shook his head in despair. "He's going to kill us all."

"The Führer? Dr. Rudi?" I pulled his head to my shoulder and wrapped my arms around him.

He rubbed my belly where our baby was growing. "How is he supposed to grow up in this kind of world where we kill people to help them fight and kill others for us?"

"I don't know. We'll just have to do our best and hope that all this violence doesn't set into our precious child." There was no way I could keep our child safe when it got to his or her teens. The government would make them join Hitler's Youth, and all their innocence would be gone.

It wasn't the time to tell my dear husband that we could leave if we wanted to. He might not like what he'd seen today, but it wasn't enough for him to leave his military career behind.

• • • • ● ● • ● ● • •

Our beautiful boy, Will, had been born early and was healthy. He was everything a first-time mother could have asked for. He didn't cry, and seemed to enjoy listening to things in the office those first few months.

At the risk of having a complaint made to the Gestapo that I wasn't doing my duty, I dropped my little boy off at his grandparents', which they loved.

While I hated leaving my baby with someone else, it was a relief to be able to run errands during lunch that would have taken twice as long with a baby in tow.

Ernst urged Wilhelm to join him every Sunday for visits out to Dr. Rudi's home, where discussions and demonstrations were conducted for some of the senior staff.

"Wilhelm, you must consider that being with these men will help to motivate you to new heights in our great new state being built. They will notice you, and when someone is needed for a new opening, yours will be one of the first names they mention. It could be so good for you, and the family, of course."

Poor Wilhelm would give in, even though he was exhausted, and simply wanted to spend time with us.

"I'm sure you understand what a great opportunity this is for him, sister. Just imagine yourself in the home of someone who didn't deserve it anymore. All those rooms for you and my nephew to live in, while Wilhelm here is promoted." He pinched the baby's cheek, making him cry.

I couldn't say what I really wanted to, because that would have meant I wasn't a loyal German. If only my brother hadn't turned into such a monster.

Each time Wilhelm returned from one of those forced visits, he would become more withdrawn. It would take days before he could smile again. And when I asked him about what was going on, he refused to tell me.

"I won't mention such terrors to my pregnant wife," he'd always say, as if to encourage his resolve. "I just have to ignore what's happening out there."

With this pregnancy, I grew round a little faster, and allowed Ernst to convince me that I should take some time off until the baby came.

While I normally wouldn't have given in on something like that, it was harder than my first pregnancy, and I was almost certain it was a girl.

Almost all of my activities for the resistance had been halted due to the fact that I wasn't in a position to direct supplies to them. The doctor was afraid I might be in danger of losing the baby during the last few weeks and recommended bedrest.

I felt so helpless during those days, lying in bed, but that gave me the time I needed to complete my plans of getting my family to safety.

In case the worst happened, I knew I needed to tell Wilhelm there was an option for him and the children to escape. So, one night, I laid my fears to rest and confided in my husband.

"Dearest, I know you've been really upset at the things going on at Dr. Rudi's, and I have a way for you and babies to get out if anything happens to me. You can't let the children be raised here, where my brother will be one of their main influences." I thought appealing to his protective side might be the best way to get him to go along with my plan.

"You're a loyal German, but sometimes we have to do things that are considered dishonest, simply to protect those we love." I took his hand in mine and held it to my stomach, just as the baby kicked. "We have to think about our family. And if the circles under your eyes are any indication of the evil, these men have planned, then we need to have a plan ready."

To my utter amazement, he agreed.

"I don't want to know the details, but if something happens to me, I want you to have a way out of the country. Your brother is determined to draw me into this pit of hell, and I don't see any way for me to escape." He bowed his head, the thought of failing me simply too much for him to bear.

"You have to come with us. It won't be the same without you. I don't want to have to tell the children their uncle was the cause of their father's death."

"If anything happens to you, I promise to take the children and leave, but you must promise me the same. I couldn't bear knowing I wasn't here to protect you from you him. He'll try to marry you off again to anyone who can help further his career." He shuddered at the thought of the men my brother would try to pair me up with.

"So no, I don't care how much it costs or if it's illegal. I want our family to survive. There's no way that can happen if you stay here. Horrible things are coming, and no one should have to see that."

We didn't talk about it again after baby Hope was born, but each of us quietly put together the supplies we'd need to take with us if we left. That was when I decided to start teaching the children English, German, Russian, and French.

Since we only spoke German with extended family, I hadn't been worried that it would be a problem until one day, when Ernst was over to escort Wilhelm to his dinner.

Will was just starting to walk and say random words out loud. He spoke the same word in all four languages, as if trying to make sure he'd used the right one. I couldn't scold him for doing what I'd been teaching him.

"Really, Thea? Do you have to teach them those horrible languages?" he scoffed at me. "He won't have any use for them since we're going to make all our conquered countries speak German. Then again, you were always a dreamer, sister. Maybe he can help us interrogate the prisoners so we know what they're trying to say in their inferior languages." He laughed at the horrified look on my face. "Don't worry. We'll make good little Nazis out of them."

As the door closed behind him, I slid to the floor and clutched my babies to my chest. I couldn't let him near my children; he was going to get them killed.

Wilhelm came home that day and went straight to the small cubicle he deemed an office, and stayed in there for several hours.

Finally, he came into the kitchen, where I was warming up something for dinner.

"Thea, it's time we talked about our future." His serious tone made my stomach drop to my feet.

"When the babies are asleep, we'll consider our options," I answered mechanically.

He only nodded and took a seat.

Throughout dinner, we both avoided looking at each other, mostly moving the food around on our plates.

I laid both Hope and Will in their cribs with a kiss as my heart felt broken due to the plans we were about to make.

• • • ● ● • ● ● • • •

Things hadn't happened as easily, nor as quickly as I'd planned. Momma had gotten sick, and I'd had to leave the babies with one of the help while I stayed by her bedside, as she declined within a few short months.

Her funeral was a simple affair, attended by close friends and family, but the strain of trying to care for my family and Mother all at once had taken a toll, and I'd fainted at her service.

I'd awakened to find the family doctor standing over me as I laid in the bed in my parent's house. I rose, but he eased me back down.

"No need to hurry, my dear. You've worn yourself out caring for your mother. You really need to take better care of your health, and that of the baby."

"Baby? I'm pregnant? I have a nine-month-old. That's too soon," I protested.

"Well, my dear, there isn't really any way to take it back. Plus, it's another little one to help grow our Fatherland," he replied proudly.

"Sorry, I'm just in shock. Of course, it's such a blessing with the passing of my mother and everything. I just wasn't expecting this so soon." I looked up, worried he would report my negative response to this child.

He patted my shoulder. "Don't worry. Once you get some rest and eat properly, you'll feel better. Take it easy for a while and take care of those babies. I don't want to have you back in my office every couple of days."

"No, sir, I won't be. I just wore myself down with taking care of Mother. I didn't want her to suffer."

His smile helped to calm me down. "I'm going to tell them I gave you something to help you sleep, and that you should stay here until the morning." He paused with his hand on the door and gave me a wink. "I won't tell the expectant father about the baby. I'll let you share that joyous news."

I nodded, trying not to cry at his kindness. "Thank you."

Guilt overwhelmed me as I thought about how worried Wilhelm would be. I'd have to make it up to him, I promised as my eyes drooped, unable to keep them open.

• • • ● ● ● ● ● ● • •

I never got the chance to, because my brother showed up a few days later.

"Hey, sis. I'm here to tell Wilhelm that we'll be leaving in the morning."

"Leaving? Where are you taking him?" The words left my mouth before I could think about the wisdom of questioning him.

"He's about to see how the mighty German army's newest weapon works on the Russians. It's about time one of our heroes returned to where the action is, and does more for our country than knock you up," he snickered as

I held onto nine-month-old Hope, with Will clinging to my legs.

"For the good of the Reich, of course. When do you leave?" I knew our future had just been decided for us.

"In the morning. We're on our way to Demyansk in Russia, where they've been having trouble. With our new weapon, we're going to completely demoralize them."

"Oh, well, I'm sure that'll be exciting. Just bring him back to me, please. That's all I ask of you."

He tilted his head, as if he was considering it. "Of course, my dear sister. I would hate for you to lose two people in such a short time. Give Wilhelm this packet. It has all the information he'll need for our trip." He tossed the large envelope on the table with a thud. "See ya."

Our lives changed in that moment, and I had no idea what I was going to do about it.

• • • • ● • ● ● • • •

"I can't go with you," Wilhelm continued to argue as we discussed our options again. "You simply have to leave. No one will know where you've gone or why until it's too late to do anything about it." He gripped my hand tightly. "Now, I've sewn the documents into the bottom of the diaper bag, so if you're searched, no one will mess with it. It will give the English an advantage on how to kill these things if they'll take it seriously."

"This baby won't even know who you are." I cried. It wasn't rational, but the baby hormones were doing things to my body. "I can't survive without you."

He pulled me into his lap. "Sure you can. Where's the girl who wasn't going to get married just because she'd been told to? You are so much stronger than you give yourself credit for."

"You know my brother will kill you when he realizes that I'm gone, right?"

"No, he won't, because you're going to tell everyone you're visiting the country, but you won't ever arrive. No one would blame you for needing a little peace and quiet after your mother's death."

"My brother isn't going to be happy that I'm gone," I protested, worried about what was going to happen.

"You can drop me a letter, and when I get home, I'll be just as surprised as he is that you're gone. Then we can both look for the people who took you." He grinned. "I might not be happy about going to the Russian front, but I'm going to enjoy the look on your brother's face when he has to find you."

We spent the rest of the afternoon together until it was time for bed.

I was asleep when Wilhelm left the next morning, but the emptiness I felt was still with me two months later as I lay here on this bed in England without him by my side.

It had taken a few days to orchestrate the moving of the children and me with the family and servants. The country home had to be cleaned, and they needed to get there before we did so we could disappear.

I packed everything of value and had taken it to my father's to be stored. Everything looked and appeared as if we were just going for an extended stay in the country to get away from it all for a while.

The network I'd helped to establish so others like the Rosenblatts could make it out of the country, gave me the opportunity to leave without harming me or the children.

Several boat voyages, and stays with families in small quarters, had all accumulated with us arriving in time to hear about the battle in Demyansk.

I could only hope he'd survived whatever evil deeds my brother and Dr. Rudi had planned for the poor men on the battlefield in Russia.

A tear slid down my face as I drifted off to sleep, cuddled up to my two precious children.

CHAPTER NINE

RUDI

The day had finally arrived for me to test out my wonderful little weapons. I'd stopped calling them humans years ago, as that seemed to hold more of a bad taste than simply "weapons." People would get squeamish if they thought we were testing dead humans as the newest form of an attack on our enemies.

Not that I really cared what anyone would think, but still, polite society needed the illusion that I wasn't doing anything nefarious.

Several boxcars had been filled with my subjects and given the serum. If the growls coming from the compartments were any indication, they were ready to take on the Russians.

"Guten morgen, Doctor," Ernst greeted me with his brother-in-law in tow.

"Guten morgen to you, Major. I see you brought our favorite oberleutnant with you." I gave each of them a salute so they didn't feel slighted.

I hadn't felt the need to join the army, but I'd done more than any general had to help our side win the war. Not many civilians could say that about themselves and be truthful in telling that tale.

Ernst's smile masked what I knew to be a devious mind that rivaled my own. "Is your ammunition ready to travel?"

"Ja. We are ready to board the train." I motioned for them to climb on board ahead of me.

"Very good." Ernst took one of the more comfortable seats, leaving the other for me, while his brother-in-law took one of the empty bench seats.

"This has been a long time in coming. I'm just sad you're the only representative who is going to see my masterpieces," I complained, dropping into my seat.

"Ah, Rudi, not everyone can handle the battlefield, or Russia, for that matter. If this works, then everyone will know of your success. Then again, if it doesn't..." He let his words hang in the air. We all knew it would be a swift death.

"Well, I'm very sure of my superior weapons. They'll do what they're supposed to do, don't you worry. I've spent years perfecting these things to fight for us," I boasted proudly of my project.

The only unease I felt about things going the way they were supposed to was if the train actually made it to Russia. We'd brought another two boxcars of prisoners to drag the other boxcar where we needed it. Then, they would be the bait we sent toward the Russians. All we would have to do is stand back and let nature take its course.

Ernst filled the next few hours with idle chitchat, and it was only when his snores filled the car that I could think properly again.

Wilhelm looked like he would rather be anywhere else than in the car with the two of us.

I stood to stretch and made my way over to him.

"Mind if I have a seat with to you?"

"Uh, no." He moved his feet and tried to brush away any leftover dirt.

"I find that I crave the company of people after working with the dead for hours on end. Do you think my weapons won't work?" I eyed him carefully to see what the problem might be.

He blushed, looking flustered. "No, sir. I don't like the idea of using humans to fight against our enemy. There has to be another way to win battles and this war."

"You would think so, but I've found that demoralizing them works so much better. If they hear rumors of troops willing to run through bullets to tear their throats out, they'll flee before our army. If the enemy has nightmares of being eaten alive, only to return as the undead, they won't be as willing to fight us." I enjoyed the grimace, he couldn't hide at my words.

"No offense, sir. It just doesn't seem very honorable." He shrugged, as if voicing his reluctance wouldn't be a death sentence for most men.

"Thank you for your honesty. We did a good job during the Great War, and if I had been able to create their predecessors earlier, we might not have had to surrender. This time, with the tweaks I've made to the virus, there will be no stopping us."

"You sound so confident. I wish I could be so sure. What if these weapons, or rather, Storm Troopers, as you're calling them, escape the parameters and start attacking villages? There's no way to contain these things after we let them loose," he protested with the same argument many before him had argued.

"The difference is that we know how to kill them. The enemy had to use mustard gas in the last war, which hurt their own men. Now they'll take bullets and keep on going. We've equipped them with helmets resistant to bullets, so a headshot is much more difficult to manage. They'll have to physically fight them to have a chance to survive."

"How are we going to keep them from overpowering our troops?"

"Good question. If we lose a few troops to gain major military advantages, then I consider those to be acceptable losses." I smiled. "Just wait, you'll see how wonderfully this will all work."

He still didn't look convinced, but wisely kept his mouth shut.

• • • ● ●• ● ● • •

The train arrived at our destination in the middle of a blizzard. Russia was so damn cold this time of year.

I'd come prepared for it, though, and got everything ready for our departure as soon as the snow stopped swirling.

"Don't open those cars until we've advised the military what's going to happen," I warned the soldiers milling about the temporary station that had been erected.

They didn't know any of the secret orders that I carried, but it didn't matter what they thought, because I had the full approval of the Führer. No one would dare go against his instructions.

By mid-afternoon, the storm had cleared, and we were prepared to have everything ready for the morning's battle.

I rubbed my hands together in anticipation. This was going to be glorious.

Just before dawn, all of the troops were withdrawn quietly and moved to the area behind the train that had been built to withstand the assault of the dead in case they malfunctioned.

I hadn't been able to close my eyes all night, waiting for this moment. "Are we ready?"

"Yes, Doctor. Should we let the weapons out?" Ernst questioned eagerly.

"Proceed. Make sure only those of you who must be out do so. Everyone else needs to be safely behind the barricade."

I took up my position in the railcar and held the binoculars to my face. I wanted to be able to see everything that happened as it unfolded before my eyes.

The sun began to rise as the sounds of growls filled the air. A few soldier volunteers—and I used that word loosely—held open the doors to the prisoners' compartments.

Whistles blew, and the prisoners walked until the doors opened with weapons trained on the cars, and they realized that something was going to kill them.

They took off running through the snow without coats as the dead started to chase them.

I stood there as they fanned out, with many of the dead overtaking them and turning them quickly.

Gunfire rang out as the few remaining prisoners and dead reached the Russian soldiers.

The battle was epic, but was over very quickly. All that was left were the dead munching on the corpses that hadn't reanimated yet.

"Send in the first group of our soldiers to start corralling them back to the last two train cars," I ordered.

Noise seemed to attract my weapons, and the bells and whistles on the train rang until they were gathered hungrily around the cars with slats that let the smell of the living out.

My wave had the men on top of the car opening the door to let them back inside. As the last one entered, they hurried to shut the doors behind the dead.

"Send the soldiers in, and make sure the fortifications are strong enough to keep the Russians from retaking this area," I ordered as the train engine arrived to take us back to Germany.

"That's it?" Ernst declared. "How do we know if it worked? Did you count the amount of dead that got back into the car?"

"No. The soldiers we've just sent out will tell us if we were successful. You don't hear guns firing, do you?" I took my seat, satisfied that I'd done what I set out to do. "That means they accomplished their goal and the Russians are dead."

Ernst turned away in disgust over not being able to personally see the outcome, while Wilhelm stayed quiet, watching our soldiers run toward the battlefield with bayonets to make sure any of the dead stayed that way.

"What was the point in all this?" he asked, feeling my gaze on him.

"A practice run to make sure it works. We're going to need an advantage if the Allies make a landing on the shores of France. They beat us there with the sheer amount of men they could continue to send against us. This time, we're doubling our army." I couldn't wait to get started on my serum for mass production.

"Any time one of our men dies in certain units, he'll turn into one of the undead. I've changed the virus enough that he's focused on aggressively taking out anything in uniform. We'll have men stopping an invasion, and as a last measure, they'll wreak havoc on the enemy."

I pulled Ernst's chair close to mine and put my feet up. I'd been awake and running on little sleep for days, and now I could finally rest before the actual fun began by helping to win the war for my country this time.

"God help us," Wilhelm whispered, aghast at the possibilities that were planned for our enemies.

"He won't be able to help them, Oberleutnant. He won't be anywhere around, and the devil will be waiting to take them to hell with him."

Part 3

June 6th, 1944
D-Day Invasion with the Allied Army

CHAPTER TEN

— · —

RUDI

The Allied forces were supposed to be landing somewhere in the next few days, and I was prepared for it. My Storm Troopers, as the generals had nicknamed them, were ready to be used somewhere. It hadn't seemed right to use them in small battles, because word might have leaked to the Allies that we had a secret weapon to use. We needed the element of surprise to be on our side so we could win against these invaders.

"They were the perfect specimens," I thought aloud, admiring my handiwork again from the enclosed cages they were contained in.

"Jawohl! You have done a great service for your country. Is there anything else you require?" General Otto Adolph commended.

I simply hated when they were trying to butter me up, but this time, I couldn't help but agree with him. If these

Storm Troopers performed in the same manner that my others on the Russian front had, then there won't even be an Allied invasion. We'd take care of the problem even before they made it to the shoreline.

"No, I'm good. I would like to find a place where I can watch them perform. Is there somewhere we won't be in harm's way?" I queried.

"One of the cliffs has been built so we can monitor all of the beach. We've connected the tunnels to make it easier for us to remain out of sight from scouting planes."

The idea of being underground again didn't make me happy in the least, but if I wanted a chance to see my beauties perform, then I was going to have to compromise my own comforts.

"Very well," I agreed.

The Allied invasion was imminent, but it could still be days, weeks, or months from now. I could only hope that things would go according to plan instead of screwing things up like they had been in Russia. The generals had not been happy that my weapon had taken out a section of our own troops who hadn't gotten the message to return to the temporary station.

We, of course, blamed the losses on the Russians, but that didn't mean they were going to continue to let our men die instead of the enemy.

Thank the gods, it had been considered a success, due to the fact that we had obliterated the Russians in the battle of Demyansk. That was one of the reasons I'd gotten the go ahead for this project to continue.

Only time would tell if I was a genius or one of those failed scientists shot for his crimes.

CHAPTER ELEVEN

CAMERON

Today was the day we'd been preparing for all this time—the biggest invasion in history against a common enemy.

It was still dark on the English shore as we lined up with our units to load up the ships that would send us to face what would hopefully be the last big battle of the war.

Pope sat beside me as we crouched down to keep the sea spray out of our faces. While the trip across the channel wasn't supposed to take that long, we were loading under the cover of night to avoid alerting the Germans that we were coming. Their planes continued to bomb London, and I personally didn't want to take a chance on them dropping a bomb on our transport while we were out at sea.

There was an air of anticipation amongst the troops and our unit, as we were finally going to battle against those who were bent on destroying homes and lives.

"You think we'll actually get to kill Germans this time?" Booth asked from the other side of Pope.

"I hope so," I murmured as the gate closed, pulling us into the queue. "I'm sure they know something's going on, and it's only a matter of time before they try to rain fire down upon us."

Whereas I'd once been someone who could see the bright side of things, these days, I was certain that death waited around the corner for each of us.

The mail hadn't been running as often, and the letters I'd received from Irene were the only ray of hope I had left to hold on to. She still thought I was somewhere in the dessert, but slowly, all of the troops had been brought closer to England to await this day.

While I had no aspirations that she genuinely cared for me, I was hopeful maybe someday, if we both made it out alive, we could explore the possibility of a future. Until then, I just needed to keep my head down and dodge any and all bullets that were aimed in my direction.

Easier said than done, I thought as another plane droned by overhead, causing all of us to duck down a little farther into the transport.

I knew I should rest, but for the first time in weeks, we were actually doing something. The adrenaline was making it hard to settle down and focus on anything but the next step.

In my letter to Irene, that I'd composed in case something happened to me, I'd shared my thoughts on the coming battle.

Irene,

I wrote only two days ago, but as I'm sure you know, there is something brewing for our division. We don't know exactly where or when, but we are about to move onto occupied soil. Since you work for one of the generals, you probably already know where I'm going to be before I do. I hope that means you'll know if I make it or not, because I don't want you to be left not knowing how it turns out for me in the end.

With the future undecided, I'm hoping we can use these moments to simply live. It's so strange, considering the fact that we are in a war that might kill us in the very next instant. This is what I signed up for, though. If by some strange chance, my death, injury, or survival help to end this war, then I'll be happy whatever the outcome.

Sorry this letter has gotten so morose, but if we make it through, could we go out on a date?

Yeah, you don't have to answer me now. In case I do survive, know I'm still interested in the future.

Anyway, I've rambled long enough. There isn't really a reason for me to continue except to say—stay safe.

Cameron

The letter was with a trusted friend who was willing to hold all of our goodbye letters just in case we didn't make it back.

It was all beginning to get to me: the long months, make that years, away from home. The moments where we'd come together as a unit fighting down in the desert, but this still felt like the start of a new school day. We had troops that had arrived in England only days ago, with no idea how to fight or what it would mean to be part of the action. Thankfully, they were paired with units of more seasoned troops that would help keep them alive just a little longer.

The transport boat shifted with the waves and doused us again with a salty spray every few minutes on what would have been a quick trip across the channel, except for the fact that we were going in a line.

Honestly, I had no idea how the Allied forces had gotten so many men onto boats and out to sea in just a few short hours. They were certainly organized in their plans. Now, we just had to survive the sea so we could face German bullets with the coming dawn.

• • • • • • • • • •

The Germans had either found out we were coming, or decided they were going to strafe any ships close to shore, because after the halfway point, it appeared we were their targets. Aircrafts continued to make passes over our open boats, making cover nearly impossible.

Bullets were going to be the least of our problems as we tried to unload through the water to get a foothold on the beach. At least we weren't the only ones in this fight, but I couldn't spend time worrying about how the British troops were faring when the gate hit the ground, meaning we were up next to unload onto the beach called Omaha.

All of us scrambled to get our gear together as we lined up to take our chances on the beach against an enemy that needed to be wiped out.

Another plane flew overhead, which had us ducking instinctively, as if getting smaller would make us less of a target.

"Asses out! Move faster, and don't leave anyone behind. It's important you keep moving, as the sea wants you dead just as much as the Germans do. Show them what you're made of!" our platoon sergeant Pittman yelled over the sound of the motors and gunfire.

"Here we go", I muttered. Jumping off the ramp into the waist deep water made me gasp at its cold temperature.

Holding my rifle over my head to help keep it dry, I pushed against the waves, making a little bit of progress toward the beach. It was still dark, with hints of color beginning to lighten the sky as we made our way closer to shore.

The urge to flop onto the ground and catch our breath was powerful, but between the planes strafing us with gunfire, and the German machine guns adding to the overall confusion, it was obvious we had to keep going toward something. Not that any of us were exactly sure where that something was located.

"This way!" Sergeant Pittman waved, standing bravely at the front to direct us to him. He was a target for gunfire while making sure we all made it in from the water to relative safety.

As we dripped our way across the beach, sand clinging to our wet clothes, we gathered behind one of the dunes hidden from the guns for a short time to regroup.

I watched in amazement as hundreds of black dots filled the sand, making it look like an army of ants trying to flow onto the beach from the ocean. Each one of those dots was a person who was going to help us win this war.

"Men, I need you to move around this dune and try to take that small hill so we can begin to establish a perimeter for those coming out of water." He motioned toward what was almost a small mountain rather than a hill.

"You want us to climb that?" Pope asked in disbelief. "Guess we might as well get started. You're going to cover my ass, right, O'Malley?"

Without waiting for me to answer, he jumped out and started running toward the bottom of the hill, showing no fear. The rest of us followed a little more cautiously, making sure we weren't going to be ambushed.

In a superhuman move, Pope took a running jump to fling his body halfway up, groping for traction with his hands.

Quickly scaling his way up to the top, he landed on his stomach and looked around before throwing a rope down to the rest of us.

Three others made the climb and sent down the large rope nets that would keep our guys moving toward the goal—a foothold on land so we could fight the Germans.

We'd already worked hard as hell and needed a break, but that wasn't going to happen today unless we were dead. Then, we'd have all the time in the world.

With that grim thought running through my head, I started moving toward the back of the line where we were watching out for a surprise attack.

More men climbed up each minute, and the plateau was filling up fast. We needed to move farther out so we could find some cover.

"Pope, you take O'Malley, Booth, and Anderson over that ridge! Knock out that machine gun nest so that when they land on the beach, we won't lose them to a hail of bullets!" he yelled, then ordered another unit to go to the right.

The faster we pushed inland and cleaned out all the German nests, the sooner we would be able to make some progress and start a base camp.

I headed out with Pope, only to find there were three different hotspots that needed to be taken care of, and quickly, if the amount of rapid fire coming from them was an indication of the problem they were creating for the men on the beach.

One group noticed us creeping toward them and turned their attention, and their bullets, toward us, halting our progress.

"How are we going to get past those?" I yelled, not realizing I'd gotten louder trying to be heard above the chaos.

Pope smiled and held up a grenade. "Cover me."

Again, he didn't wait for a response, but took off running in a zigzag formation toward the first turret. The only way we were going to stop those guns was to throw a few grenades into their little foxholes, but it had to be done from a very close proximity, so the target was hit.

Not about to let him down, I took aim and fired toward the small hole that held a human on the other side.

Explosions ripped through the air as the grenades began to hit their targets, killing the machine guns. The momentary silence was deafening compared to all the noise. I was certain I'd lost my hearing, but Pope's victory yell cut through the illusion.

"Whoo!" He did a dance on the smoldering ruins before moving into the small space. "I think there's a tunnel system down here."

The others hurried to catch up with us before I slid into the still smoking hole.

We were in enemy territory and had to be careful. There could be a group of Germans simply waiting for us to show up so they could slaughter us.

Instead, it was eerily silent down below the surface where the fighting was happening. All of the tunnels appeared connected, which would be great if we could continue on to their main sleeping quarters.

I used the radio before we went too far inside, needing to get an update to Sergeant Pittman.

"Come in, Sarge. Unit 3584, reporting mission accomplished. We've found the rats' tunnels, and are proceeding with caution. If you can send more men to us, that would be helpful."

"Roger that, O'Malley. The rest of the platoon is headed in your direction. Wait until we arrive," he instructed.

"Sir, that's going to be difficult, because Pope's already making his way farther inside."

I could have sworn I heard the sergeant let out a huge sigh.

"Proceed with caution and mark your direction. We'll be along shortly."

Pope had been standing at the turnoff, and overhearing Pittman, took some chalk and put an arrow for the direction we were going to take, which led farther down into the small mountain area.

Nothing popped out at us, but the more we crept inside the tunnel, the stronger I felt that this wasn't going to turn out good for us.

Screams erupted behind us, which blocked us from retreating if we ran into trouble. Instead, we began to run forward, right into a steel door.

"What do we do now?" Booth questioned as he appraised it.

"We could blow our way inside." Anderson grinned, holding up the C4 he'd kept dry.

I shook my head at the suggestion. "Then they'll know exactly where we are. If we aren't careful, it could blow up the mountain right on top of us. We can't take that kind of chance."

"Those screams aren't getting any better, so I don't think we can go backward," Pope tried to reason for the more dangerous option.

"More reason to go back and help our unit and friends."

Growls joined the screams echoing through the tunnels, making it seem like they were just moments from being on top of us.

"Go ahead." I motion to Anderson reluctantly. "We've got to clear all of this area, and hopefully those behind us have more support coming from the surface."

Placing the C4 didn't take long. We ducked around the corner, hoping it would shield us from most of the fallout.

The walls trembled with the force of the blast, but they stayed in place as we checked around the corner to see that the door was gone.

Dust and smoke were the only things that moved in the dim lights hanging from the ceiling.

"Yes!" Pope gave Anderson a fist bump. "Let's do this."

He took off, barely holding his gun in front of him as he charged through the door and into the enemy's unknown world.

The radio buzzed, but the only thing that came through was a blip with some static.

Unable to let them know we were going deeper, I heaved off the wall, glad for the few moments of rest before walking into the enemy's quarters.

• • • ● ● • ● ● • •

We weren't prepared for what was behind the door. Cages lined the walls, filled with what looked like dead people.

The place was a horror show, and we were smack dab in the middle of it.

Pope had disregarded the need for stealth and had turned on the light, illuminating the horrors in front of us.

He jumped back, almost landing in my arms. "What the hell is that?"

"Dead people, or zombies. Maybe dead zombies?" I offered, moving closer to the cages.

These zombies were dead. Someone had shot them, but it was difficult to tell when it had happened, because they looked fresh still, and gooey.

Anderson shuffled nervously, holding his gun at the ready in case they jumped out at us. "We need to get out of here."

"Hold on," I cautioned, pushing past a shocked Pope until I was standing next to the cages. "One of them may not be dead after all."

A groan confirmed my fears as I watched one of the bodies begin to move out from under the other corpses.

"Let's go back to the surface. I'd rather face bullets than whatever those things are," Booth urged, edging toward the tunnels we'd just come from.

"No, we can't. Remember those growls we heard? I'm going to bet there are more of these things filling the tunnels. We've got to push on and make sure there aren't any more of them wandering around. At least we know what to look for, while the others don't know what to expect."

Pope, who was normally the most fearless person I knew, was almost pale in the florescent lights.

"Look, I don't want to be here anymore than either one of you do. Sarge sent us down here to take out the enemy, and that's what we've got to do. Imagine if these things made it up to the surface. A bullet in the head is what killed these zombies." Wanting to prove my theory, I pointed my gun at the forehead of the one that was still trying to unpin itself and squeezed the trigger.

The sound echoed off the walls as the zombie fell back against the floor, and all signs of movement ceased.

"Yep, a bullet between the eyes will take it out. We'll use our pistols so we can aim a little better, but we've got to keep going."

"Hell, man, this isn't right, but someone's got to do it. Let's find a way out so we can report back to the Sarge," Booth agreed reluctantly.

This time, I took the lead and went down the dim hallway. It had some bulbs hung along the walls, which didn't provide much in the way of light, but it was enough that we could see if something was up ahead.

Each hallway appeared to be leading farther down into the mountain. There was no way of knowing when we'd be walking into the enemy.

Voices echoed through the tunnels, so I put my hand up and whispered, "Stop."

We clustered together quickly, while keeping an eye out to make sure we weren't going to be ambushed from behind.

"I think we've found where they've been living. It's up ahead. If we use our guns, it's going to alert every German within miles of here," I cautioned.

"What do you suggest if we can't use our guns? I'm not going up against one of those things with my bare hands."

I shook my head. "You're right, but let's use them only in extreme circumstances. There are only four of us, and a lot more of the enemy milling about here. They know where they're going, and we're more likely to get lost than to find our way back out to the top."

They all nodded, and we assumed positions as we started toward the voices.

"I can't believe they want us to let those things out," someone commented from around the corner.

"Just be glad they're on our side. Those guys won't last long, but at least they'll take out some of the enemy while they're at it. Although, I'm not sure I'd wish that kind of death on the enemy. It seems like a really bad way to die," another voice replied.

"After we've set these charges, we can get out of here and let the super soldiers do what they were created for."

I exchanged glances with the others. "This wasn't good. How could we warn our troops? Better yet, how could we stop them?"

Making a split-second decision, I stepped into view.

"Heil Hitler!" As expected, both men snapped at attention, allowing me to point my gun at them.

While we'd been waiting the past few weeks on board the ships and desert, I'd been trying to learn German so I could use it if necessary.

"I don't want to kill you. I just need to know the best way to the surface," I spoke rapidly, hoping I was saying it correctly.

They pointed to the door in front of them without answering.

"Pope, you want to do the honors?" If they were telling the truth, then we might be able to radio our group and send a few grenades down here to destroy the enemy. If not, we were dead anyway, so there wasn't much to lose in this situation.

Nodding, he scooted past the two prisoners to the door. "Ready?"

"As ready as we'll ever be." I motioned to the door, while Anderson kept watch behind us.

He threw it open with a clang, and sunlight flooded inside the dark tunnels.

Fresh air felt so good, but I was worried about what we would do with our two prisoners. We weren't equipped to hold on to them, but if we let them go, they would alert someone.

"What are we going to do with these guys?" Booth questioned, looking around nervously.

"Nothing. They've set charges, and I'm pretty sure this thing is going to blow up at any minute."

Switching to German, I poked them with the butt of my gun. "When is it going to explode?"

They glanced at each other and held up five fingers.

"Five minutes?"

With a unified nod, I had to trust it was the truth. With a tilt of my head, I motioned for them to run.

There was no point in killing someone when they were doing what we wanted them to do, anyway. Why were they blowing up their own tunnels?

"I think we need to get back to the others and alert them that all hell is about to break loose," I warned, heading toward the beaches and gunfire at a run.

"Huh?" Pope yelled as he and the others fell into step beside me.

"They're blowing up their own crap so those things can get out. I don't know what they do, but it's not going to be good. We need to let everyone know."

"Aw, shit!" Pope yelled, tearing down the mountain ahead of us.

We reached the edge of what we thought was the beach, but it was a different section, probably miles from where we started. There were no Germans or Allied troops below us, but we could hear the screams from farther down the beach.

Somewhere in all the tunnels, instead of going toward the middle, we'd made our way up and over. It would cost us precious minutes to find a way back to our platoon. That was, if we didn't come across more of the enemy along the way.

Anderson kicked at the ground in frustration. "Crap. Now, what are we going to do?"

"The radio might be our only option." Booth pulled his out. "Sergeant Pittman, this is Booth. Please, come in."

"Booth, where the hell are you? We tried to follow you and got overrun by these... these things!"

"Yes, sir, we know. That's why we're calling, because the place is full of them. The Germans are about to blow it up, and then they're going to be everywhere."

"Great." Sergeant Pittman added a few more words that were lost in translation. "Get your asses back here ASAP. We're going to pull back."

"Roger. We'll be there when we can."

"You heard the man. We need to hoof it. Plus, I don't really want to be standing here when this mountain explodes under our feet." I started running along the edge of the cliff, looking for a place we could slide or climb down without being killed.

We had barely gotten our feet onto the sand when the first blast sent parts of the mountain raining down around us.

Already out of breath, we made it to the water and out of reach of the falling rocks, only to see huge numbers of what looked like the undead swarming out of the newly made holes from the explosion.

"This just went from bad to worse!" Booth yelled as we tried to figure out what to do next.

A small fishing boat approached, and since they weren't firing on us, I was going to take that as a good sign they were on our side.

"Do you boys need a lift back over to the main fight?" A long-haired fisherman with a full beard asked with a twinkle in his eyes.

He didn't have to ask twice before we were scrambling into the boat.

"What are those things coming out of the mountain?" He squinted in the direction of the dead, which looked like small ants as we pulled away.

"The turning point in today's battle," I muttered, knowing we had just lost a lot of lives.

With a frown, he urged his little motor faster, thinking he'd missed something important.

As we rounded the corner, the fighting became more intense, and we were still sending troops onto shore, even though the threat was growing.

"Do you see our guys anywhere?" Anderson covered his eyes from the sun as he scanned for someone who looked familiar in the massive group of camouflaged bodies.

"We're just going to have to find the command base and alert them to what's about to come at them." I shook my head. "If this is just those who are still alive, I can't imagine the damage those who are dead are going to do to our forces."

The little fishing boat pulled up to where our side had built a temporary landing dock so that the troop ships didn't get caught with the tide.

We hadn't even pulled out when several medics rushed up, placing several wounded inside the boat.

"Where do you need to go, boys?" the boat pilot asked, waving to us with a smile as we jumped out to deliver our warning.

By the time I glanced back over my shoulder at the end of the makeshift peer, his little boat was full of wounded, with more lining up to wait for the next boat.

"There!" Pope shouted, pointing toward what appeared to be our platoon.

Dodging bullets and running through the sand in wet clothes made it difficult to move quickly, as our progress moved slowly to the one safe zone on the beach.

"About time you showed up," Sergeant Pittman complained as we tried to catch our breath hidden behind one of the larger dunes.

"Sir, they're going to be coming around that large area toward us."

"Who?" Frowning, he rubbed at his ear, as if that would make it easier to hear.

"The dead. The Germans have managed to weaponize the dead. I don't know how it works, but we saw some that had been shot in the head. They appear dead, but will continue to move around afterward. I'm not sure what they can do to us, but I don't want to know."

Screams full of terror started to fill the air.

"When grown men scream, that's never good." He sighed heavily. "Start getting our guys back on the boats as quickly as possible.

The radio began to squawk with numerous reports all at once.

"These things are coming out of the side of the hill."

"I've been bitten! They're not shooting at us anymore, but trying to eat us!" Someone screamed into the radio

"This is worse than we could've imagined," I groaned.

Instead of using his handheld radio, Sergeant Pittman grabbed the portable that would reach the ships.

"We have a huge problem. The dead are attacking our guys. Requesting help. Over."

CHAPTER TWELVE

IRENE

I 'd been one of the general's favorite secretaries after helping Thea and her kids out, so he had requested we all be on board the ship that was going to oversee the invasion forces for our big day.

It was going to be our job to ensure he had all the messages and up-to-the minute information we could collect from the radios and enemy communications as to how things were beginning to progress.

Those of us working as his assistants had developed a type of shorthand with each other so we could sort out what was urgent and what wasn't as life-threatening.

Things hadn't been wonderful during those first hours of landing on the beaches, but we'd breached the perimeter and were making headway inland. A few hundred thousand men had been delivered along various points to the French shores so our army could pin the Germans in without allowing them a chance to escape.

Reports had been coming in consistently that we were making progress toward the inner fortifications they'd put along the beach to keep us out. Machine guns were being taken out, and our Air Force were fighting continuously overhead with the German Messerschmitt as they tried to kill as many of our guys as they could before they made it to land.

While I hated to hear about our casualties, they were going to happen. And, unfortunately, there was a certain amount that had been considered appropriate losses for this kind of offensive.

Something out of the ordinary caught my attention, though, and I listened with growing horror as I started waving frantically to get someone's attention. I couldn't put down the headset for fear I'd miss something important that could be vital to saving lives.

Clara saw my frantic attempts to get help and came over.

"What's wrong, Irene?"

"Get the general, now!" I ordered.

She took in my serious expression and raced off, flying toward the other side of the large room to get him.

"Sir, Officer Fitzgerald requests that you come over to the radio station immediately. Sir," she rushed out.

"It's urgent, I presume, Officer Higgins?"

"Yes, sir."

"Very well." He turned to the others. "We'll take this up again momentarily."

"He's going to go give a listen to the women he keeps around," one of the Brits standing around scoffed. "What do they know about a battle?"

General Eisenhower ignored the comment and arrived at my elbow as I frantically connected to another station.

"Sir, I'm not sure if you're aware of the almost fatal catastrophe that happened during the Great War when our dead began to bite and attack our troops, but my father was the doctor who was able to stop them."

"I'm aware of Fitzgerald's help during that horrible incident. Is there a point to this?" His patience was wearing thin.

"Yes, sir. It's happening again. I'm getting reports from two areas that the inside of the mountain filled with these super soldiers. They're coming back from the dead and attacking our men." I had no way of knowing if this was what Thea's information had warned him about.

"What the living hell is going on? There's no way the Germans could have known we would use these beaches for an invasion."

"No, sir, they didn't. The platoon that was supposed to clear out the mountain did so, but the Germans had wired it to explode, causing the dead to come out of the Earth. What do I tell them, sir?"

"Retreat. We can't afford to have this grow among the troops. Bring me someone who's been there, and let's work on getting our men off those beaches."

"Yes, sir." I saluted and pulled the headset back into place. "S.O.S. This is a retreat for the Omaha and Utah beaches. I repeat, begin moving back to the ships immediately."

"General," I called to his retreating form. "At the moment, the only beach affected are those on Omaha and Utah. It appears the others haven't been a problem. Should they continue inland?"

He paused before turning back to me. "Once someone can inform us of what exactly is happening on those two beaches, we'll update the others to be on the lookout for a trap of this sort. Officer Fitzgerald, do you know how to combat these soldiers?" he questioned.

"Yes, sir. A shot through the head, which is difficult considering the helmets they wear are to protect them from that very thing. Other than blowing them up, there's not much that can be done. On the other hand, if our soldiers get bitten by one of these super soldiers, then the time between the bite and death is different depending on the person. We give out the ZIV vaccine, but it hasn't been tested in battle yet. We have no idea if it will actually stop our troops from turning into these things or just slow the process."

"Very well. Issue the order to clear out the Utah and Omaha beaches. Make sure all the officers are aware that they may be fighting their own men on the way back to the ships."

"Sir?" I frowned, knowing he wasn't going to like what I was about to say. "We can't send the correct information over the radio for that. It's going to have to be a messenger delivery, or they won't take it seriously."

He slammed his fist down on the desk. "Why wouldn't they listen to me when I warned that this might be happen? Damn it, Fitzgerald, you're right. We've got to have someone on the ground coordinating this. Lieutenant General Sharp will accompany you to the command center for you to explain what we're dealing with." With a wave of his hand, the lieutenant general came to stand beside him. "You're to help Officer Fitzgerald make sure our troops are safe as they evacuate from the beaches."

"All of the invasion force, sir?" he questioned, incredulous at the thought of moving all those men within just a few hours of their arrival. "We've relocated most of the transports because of enemy fire."

"Not all of the beaches, but at least Utah and Omaha. They seem to be drawing the worst of the infected. The men won't listen to her, but they'll listen to you under my authority. Make it so."

"Yes, sir. Officer Fitzgerald, if you'll follow me." Lieutenant General Sharp snapped at attention.

"Uh..." I stood there, shocked by the turn of events. But at the thought of saving some lives, I yanked the headset off. "Yes, sir. Ready when you are."

Without another word, he took off. I rushed to follow him out to a small speedboat tied up to our battleship.

I looked down and gulped nervously as I realized I was going to have to climb down that long ladder hanging and swaying over the ocean.

His leg was already over the side when he noticed my hesitation. "Ma'am, are you going to be okay?"

My head nodded yes, but my brain screamed that I was about to die if I climbed down that ladder.

"Yep. We've got lives to save," I ground out. Following his example, I put my leg over the railing and onto the first rung of the ladder. "Hopefully, our own in the process."

• • • ● ● • ● ● • •

Nothing could have prepared me for the absolute organized chaos that was the actual battlefield. It had taken almost an hour for our small boat to make it from out in the middle of the ocean to the shores of what was being called Omaha Beach.

"Do you know where we're going?" I asked nervously, clutching a rifle to my side while trying to fasten the helmet onto my head.

"Mostly. Some of it will depend on where the main command is stationed at the moment." He hopped out of the boat and into the waist deep water before holding his hand out to me.

"Can you keep the boat in this vicinity in case we need a quick exit?" His shout to the captain seemed to float away on the waves.

"We've got to get to land before we drown." I tried to stay upright, but the pull of the ocean was strong this far out.

Holding onto each other, trying not to be swept under, we finally made it to where the water came up to our knees.

As we took a second to catch our breath, I could see the battle taking place right in front of me.

"Holy smokes!" I yelled, causing a couple of dead soldiers to look in my direction.

"Crap, we've got to get somewhere safe." Lieutenant General Sharp grabbed my arm, pulling farther up the beach to the right and out of harm's way.

"Lieutenant General, sir, I believe that the command center is over there." I pointed in the direction of the only tent on the beach that was surrounded by soldiers firing at the dead.

"Just call me LG, or Sharp. Otherwise, it's going to be confusing when we get over there," he declared as he dodged bullets while running through the sand.

I stumbled along behind him, disoriented, and not sure that either side really knew who was who. I think they'd just started firing out into the air at this point, hoping they'd hit someone.

We ducked behind a small dune.

"I've been close to a few battles, but this is crazy," Sharp informed me.

It was a wonder I could even hear with all the guns and grenades constantly going off.

"Can we make it?" I stuck my head out cautiously, trying to determine if we could make a run for the barrier the Allies were working to set up around their position.

"If we're careful, yes. We have to get back behind that set of dunes where they're climbing up the cliff."

"Agreed. Ready?" I'd caught my breath, but nothing was going to make any of this better until we were with the commanders.

We both took off running in a zigzag across the open area. Thankfully, we looked like we were alive, and those who were shooting didn't aim in our direction.

"Who's in charge around here?" Sharp yelled, looking for someone giving orders in the midst of the chaos.

"Uh, I guess I am," a weary-looking man answered as he gave someone orders. "Sergeant Pittman at your service, sir."

"Are the dead coming back to life and attacking you?" I jumped in with the question, as we didn't have time for normal army protocol.

"H–How'd you know?" he sputtered. "Never mind. Yes, they are. The damn Germans blew up their underground tunnels and let out the walking dead. These dead seem to be a little smarter than just something that wants to eat you. They're targeting those in leadership uniforms."

"You're saying the zombie things have brains? That are working?" Sharp exclaimed.

"Well, sir, that's about the only way to describe it. They're moving on from soldiers who are already dead or dying, and going for those who are commanding the troops," Pittman explained as he watched a few more men make it back to the dunes.

"So none of ours are attacking us yet, correct?"

"Correct." Pittman's head shot around to look at both of us. "Wait, what? Our own guys are going to start attacking us?"

"We're not sure." I finally caught my breath and could speak without dying. "From what happened last time, the zombie things would bite our guys, and when they died, they would come back as the thing that killed them."

"Well, crap!" Pittman threw his helmet at the ground, just as a little group of soldiers came scurrying out of the water.

"Sir, it appears that those who are injured are turning as they die," Private O'Malley sputtered.

Sharp took in the amount of troops who were still on the beach versus those who were trying to climb the cliff. "Where did these guys come from?"

"When the mountain blew up, they were deep inside the tunnels and came out as the dust settled. The Germans had this planned, and used their own men to infect with this virus before they blew up the facility," he continued, not realizing I was standing there.

"Other than trying to shoot them to make them really dead, the few I saw in the tunnels were almost alive inside, as if the person was still in there, but the body was dying. These soldiers will do anything for their Führer, and even in death, they're waging a war on us. They created the perfect little Storm Troopers that will say 'Heil' even when they're dead."

"I get that, but what do we do about them?" Pittman agreed, looking frustrated. "I've got tons of wounded from regular wounds, and now we have a new enemy that can't die to deal with?"

"Headshots should work to take them out. And from what I saw on the beach, there aren't many out there wearing headgear, so it's not totally impossible. Those who have made it up the cliff? Are the dead rising up there as well?" I questioned Pittman quickly.

"No. There aren't any of those zombie things up there yet."

"Great. Keep sending those who aren't injured up there for safety, and have them concentrate on working their way back down this area until they can shoot at these things from a safe distance. We're going to need some cover if we are to get our guys back on the boats safe." I took charge without worrying about any of their egos.

Pittman looked at me a little closer. "Who are you again?"

Cameron replied, "She's one of the WACs attached to General Eisenhower's officers."

"That's why I'm here as well, to make sure anything she says is obeyed as if the general himself was giving the order," Sharp added.

"We need to get the wounded out and keep the ground we've gained. This many soldiers can't die in vain." Determination edged my voice. "Let's try to hold this position while the others work on lining up the wounded for evacuation."

Sergeant Pittman's platoon got to work on building a ramp so we could carry the wounded out to the boats. Since the tide was starting to go out, we couldn't take a chance on one of them getting stuck.

"Triage those with life-threatening wounds first, while those who can still hold a gun need to be able to shoot at anything that comes at them. Pass the word to aim for the head, and we're going to hope for the best," I ordered, before picking up the headset and transmitting a message back to the general.

"It's as bad as we feared. Messengers need to be sent to Gold, Juno, and Sword, so they are aware of possible traps and what these super soldiers can do. We're working on saving as many wounded as possible, but Omaha Beach is covered in the dead." Hopefully, the general would understand what I was trying to convey to him.

We were sheltered under the largest tent behind a sand dune that would give us protection from the sun while keeping random bullets from hitting us.

"What about that part of the beach behind us? Why aren't we protecting our rear?" I questioned, as a plan formed in my mind.

"It's literally a solid cliff. There aren't any hidden spots on it because it's so sheer, even our best climbers can't scale it. I've got a few men over there, but unless the Germans suddenly start swimming, then I don't believe we're going to have a problem."

"Perfect, Cameron." I paused as my cheeks blushed. "Oh, excuse me, Private O'Malley. Take part of your unit and start putting our wounded under tents over there. If they've been bitten, let's get them separated and have a few of our own take turns guarding them, just in case they turn."

He grinned as he gave me a salute. "Yes, ma'am."

Booth could be heard whispering as they walked away. "That's the chick you've been writing the past few months, isn't it?"

Time seemed to stand still as we worked through all the chaos. For each thing we sorted out, another one would pop up.

The shooters on the mountaintop made a difference as they took out some of the advancing dead.

"How many could there really be out there hidden on that mountain?" Sharp shook his head in disbelief as the hoard of dead continued to come around the edge of the beach.

Hundreds, maybe thousands of our men were spread out over the five miles from the edge of the mountain back to our dune as the dead continued to advance, blocking us in.

"Can some of the troops up on the wall manage to send down some boulders to help stop them?" Pittman pointed to the edge of the cliff where more soldiers were gathering to help take out some of the advancing dead.

The radio buzzed, and we all listened to those on the front lines trying to reach us.

Even though we could see all the way down the beach, there was no way to know what was happening.

"I'm not sure who is in charge, but we've got to stop these guys from coming toward us. They're ripping into our guys and there's no way to save them. The few barricades we've got situated are being overrun." Static crackled as the voice continued. "We're going to send some of us into the hoard and try to blow them up, because we've got to stop them from coming around the beach."

His words had barely registered when a series of explosions rang through the air.

"Guess they weren't playing around with those grenades." Sharp shook his head as he picked up the mic. "Attention to all those on the cliff. Make sure you do whatever it takes to stop them from coming around the beach. We need to give our guys a break and stop the onslaught long enough for them to make some progress on a barricade."

The words hadn't even left his mouth when several German planes came roaring through the sky, raining bullets down on those trying to survive on the already besieged beachhead.

"Are there any marines we can send up the cliff to start putting some of these guys into a unit that can work from the back side of the cliff to take some of the pressure off?"

Cameron's group walked into the tent.

"We'll go," he volunteered.

Pittman protested, "O'Malley, you can't do that. You've already climbed up the cliff once today, and you've had no rest. I can't ask you to do that."

"Well, Sarge, you need us, and it's not like we're going to get a chance to sleep while those things are out there killing our brothers." Cameron shrugged like it wasn't really a big deal.

"All right." Pittman agreed. "But only because I don't have any better ideas at the moment."

"Roger that." Booth grinned, ripping the top off of some canned meat as a replacement for all the energy they were about to use.

I waited just a minute before following Cameron over to where they were sitting for a breather.

"Hey," I began shyly, unsure of how to proceed now that we were in person, and not hidden behind our letters.

"Hi," he beamed. "Gosh, you're gorgeous."

"Thanks. Not really the way I expected us to meet, but then again, we're both alive." I wanted to be positive.

"That, we are. I left you a letter just in case something happened to me. I mean, at least you'll know I was thinking about you," he stammered with a cute blush.

Booth stood up and gathered his gun. "Ready?" he asked, eyeing me with a smirk.

"Yep, in just a second." Cameron waved him off before turning to me. "I just wanted to let you know. I'd like to see you after all this is over. But, after today, I'm not sure we'll be around for that."

I placed a finger gently on his rough, dry lips. "None of that, now. We've got to believe it's going to be okay."

He started to say something, but I leaned in and kissed him instead.

"Yeah, that was more what I had in mind." Grinning, he slid an arm around me and pulled me closer for a longer kiss.

Breathless, I just stood there as he released me.

"Maybe that will be the thought that gets us through this today." With a salute, he raced to catch up with Booth, dodging bullets while trying to get to the bottom of the cliffs.

The nets were closer to the end of the beach where all the action was, and I couldn't help but feel a little bit of doom settle in as the situation became more hopeless by the minute.

· • ● ● ● • ● ● ● • ·

There was no time to think as we continued to move the wounded to an area of safety, but no matter how many we got in the line for boats, more would show up.

If there had been a moment to worry about Cameron, I would have, because the situation was more serious than any other battles so far in the war.

Sharp had been trying to keep me from going out on the front lines where the dead were attacking, but there wasn't really a way to avoid it.

They were coming closer every moment, and I wasn't paying attention when I went to help. Something grabbed at my shoulder, causing me to drop the leg of the soldier I was carrying.

A scream escaped my throat as I slid to the ground, out of its reach.

Sharp appeared with a bayonet and pierced it through the head until it stopped moving. He then held out a hand to help me off the ground.

"Guess I was acting like a girl. That was really close." I brushed off my terror as I picked up the legs of the soldier and moved him again.

When we returned to what was being called the safe zone, Sharp turned on me. "Don't go back out there again. The general would never had allowed you to come out here if he thought you would be killed by one of these things."

"I'm not going to let these men die because they're in harm's way. He would want me to save lives," I argued.

Walking over and picking up the radio, I announced, "We need every boat or fishing vessel available to come and get our wounded. They will die if we don't get help. Please, save our men," I pleaded, handing the radio back to the man I'd taken it from. "Keep sending out that call for help. It's not like the Germans don't know where we are, and we've got to get the wounded to safety."

"Yes, ma'am." He saluted and repeated the call.

"There, I've done what the general would have. We've got to get the dead, dead for good. Until that happens, there won't be a way to save our troops." I picked up my gun and walked over to the one jeep sitting in the sand. "Someone needs to lead a charge down the mountain, and I'm going to make sure that when it happens, we won't be overrun."

"What the hell are you doing?" the soldier sitting there complained as I started it up, and drove it slowly through the sand.

"Doing what you should have been doing this whole time," I remarked angrily.

It only took me a few seconds to get into position. Turning the truck sideways, I handed the keys to the stunned soldier. In a forceful tone, I ordered, "If those things start to break through, you drive back toward the tent." Climbing up on the back of the jeep, I spread my feet apart to support me. With my gun balanced on the side rail, I took aim, hitting one of the dead as it lunged for one of our men.

I looked down the sight of my gun and squeezed the trigger, dropping another one.

Sharp joined me, and it wasn't long before I couldn't hear at all.

Time passed, but all I knew was that each one of those things I took down was one less dead thing that was going to kill one of our own.

Suddenly, there was a surge of men running toward us, and Sharp touched the poor soldier in the driver's seat to head back to the command tent.

The jeep moved, and the last thing I remember was leaning against the side, trying to keep my eyes open so the dead couldn't get me.

CHAPTER THIRTEEN

WILHELM

I couldn't close my eyes after being made to watch the horrors in Demyansk. I wasn't sure what Dr. Rudi and Ernst planned to do, but I needed to request a transfer into something that wouldn't turn my stomach.

Ernst had accompanied me up to the apartment when he'd dropped me off. That's where we found the note from Thea saying she was going to the countryside for some rest before the baby was due.

"She left you all alone. Well, that means you need to come out with me this evening for dinner and a drink. No point in you batching it when you can be living it up. If I know my sister, you're going to need something new to dip your wick into while she has your little one." He gave me a suggestive wink.

"Ernst, I couldn't, really. I'm exhausted. Maybe tomorrow night after I get everything back at the office sorted out."

His smile was one of pure evil. "Didn't you know? You're not going back there. You'll be traveling with the doctor and I to the shores of France again. We've got some preparations to make before the Allies attempt to make it onto the beaches. We can't let them do that."

"Oh? No, I didn't know that. I guess a night of beer might be just the thing to cheer me up, then."

My nightmare was just beginning, and there was no way for me to escape. Day or night, the images I'd seen of those men being eaten alive were impossible to erase.

While I'd thought about using the system that Thea had fled the country with, I knew Ernst wouldn't let me go so easily. It would be better to simply go along with them and find a way to surrender to the English whenever they made it to the shores of France.

That was the only hope I had of being reunited with my family.

• • • • • • • • • •

For all of Dr. Rudi's confidence, he certainly took a long time getting things put together for the next part of his plan.

It was a month later before we began the long journey to France, and the only thing I had to hold on to was that my family hadn't been found by the Gestapo.

When we'd tried to go visit them for the weekend, once it became apparent it was going to take a little longer to gather everything that Dr. Rudi needed.

They'd never arrived, we'd been told by the servants. So, a thorough search had been conducted, only to find their car in a ravine covered in snow.

"I don't see how they could have survived for long out here." I'd broken down and cried after the search dogs hadn't found anything.

"We'll come back in the spring and see if we can find their bodies." Ernst tried to comfort me, but that just drove home the fact that my family was gone.

All I'd felt were tears of relief that they hadn't been discovered, and might be waiting for me in London.

Ernst had been convinced that I could close up the house and store all of their things at my father-in-law's home so that some other deserving German family could use the apartment.

It made the time pass by faster, but the dread at what they were planning only grew worse.

Finally, we loaded up the trucks to begin the week-long drive to the coast of France.

Under normal conditions, it wouldn't have taken quite so long, but many of the main roads had been bombed. The resistance, which no one in the German high command wished to talk about, had been very busy, and I could only hope that meant the Allies were going to start the invasion soon.

Dr. Rudi wasted no time in setting up his vaccines for the soldiers at the front. I grimaced when Ernst suggested that we both get one.

It meant that if I died; I was going to turn into something horrible, and there would be no way to warn the people around me it was about to happen.

I held my arm out, and one of his technicians found a vein before I could protest.

While I didn't feel any different, I knew what was running through my veins now. Death. There was no coming back from this. I had to make sure I made it to the English side of the battle without dying.

· · · · ● · ● · ● · · ·

My chance came sooner than I thought it would, as the preparations for an invasion began in earnest.

"There's no need for you to be among the regular soldiers. We need you on the top side in case something goes wrong to help direct our troops," Ernst strongly recommended.

"Look, you've been a wonderful brother-in-law, but things just haven't been the same since my family died. I can't continue to live like this, and I would rather my life end with a glorious death for the Führer than to waste away here. Please, let me die with my dignity intact," I tried to reason.

He let out a sigh. "Wilhelm, I've always considered you to be the brother I have never had. I don't want to stand in the way of you doing your duty. I'll be sad to lose you, but I understand."

With a quick hug, he turned and left.

Shocked that he'd actually accepted my decision, I stood there for just a moment, trying to process what had just happened.

I was free. He was going to let me die during battle, and I would get a chance to cross over to the English side.

Nothing that I had was of value here, but for the sake of appearances, I took my bag of clothing and gear over to the tunnel bunkers.

No one bothered me until an alarm sounded, alerting us that the invasion had begun.

It was go time.

● ● ● ● ● ● ● ● ● ●

I'd planned to watch most of the fight from a special spot I'd discovered. It was out of the way, and I could keep an eye out for anyone who might try to kill me.

It wasn't long before men started to land on the beaches and scatter like little bugs everywhere.

I didn't want to be labeled a coward, but at the same time, I needed a chance to get away from the very men who wouldn't hesitate to kill me if they knew what I was doing.

The reason I'd gotten a metal and was called a hero was because of my marksmanship, but I wasn't going to take a life if I could help it. Not this time.

Bullets flew, and I only had to wait for one of the men to drop to the ground before I pulled him over and out of the firefight.

He had passed out from a bullet wound to the leg. He'd live, but not if he didn't get medical attention.

Stripping off his uniform, I quickly put it on, hoping I wouldn't be discovered. Then, I wrapped his leg up tightly with my undershirt to stop the bleeding before dragging him back down to where the other Allies were gathering on the beach.

My English wasn't great, so I used a mixture of French and English to help get him on board one of the small boats. There were so many wounded and those would die without help, but I couldn't take the chance that I might get hit by a bullet and turn into one of those monsters.

"I'll help bring in some more of the wounded." When that ship left, I was determined to be on it.

Unfortunately, as I was about to stow away before they left, an explosion shook the ground under my feet.

"Good God. They've blown up the mountain," one of the men muttered under his breath.

If only they understood exactly what that meant.

Every time I'd try to get onto a boat, someone would send me off with a new set of orders to help this person or that one. I was trained to take orders, and it was hard for me to say no. If I didn't do as they ordered, they might discover I wasn't who I'd claimed to be.

Lines of soldiers waded back out to the boats, but so many needed immediate care that I didn't want to take a spot from one who might survive.

My chances of making it back to my family were growing dimmer as the hours passed. Each part of my body ached as I continued to help the wounded to safety, but that was becoming hard to do with the amount of dead attacking the living was starting to become equal.

I'd seen a woman standing on a jeep shooting for several hours, and knew that when she stopped, it was time to leave as well. For some strange reason, I felt drawn to stay nearby.

Then I saw it. One of the dead had grabbed hold of the back of the jeep and was crawling up into the space where she had sat down.

Without thinking, I threw myself on the dead, using my pistol to give it a final end.

When I walked over to where the jeep had come to a stop, the man with her came over to me.

"Thank you for saving her. Can you help me get her to that boat out in the water?" He waved toward a boat that had been idling, just out of reach.

I only nodded so my accent wouldn't give me away.

He had looped his arms under hers, and I picked up her feet so they wouldn't drag through the water.

We'd barely made it into the boat when she stirred.

"What are we doing here? Sharp?" Her tone took on a frantic quality. "I can keep helping them. Someone needs to kill more of those things."

"We're evacuating. Boats are coming to take all the wounded away, and make sure the living are out of reach. Then, we're going to bomb the entire beach," he told her.

"What about Cameron and his unit?"

"Don't worry, they're up on the cliff. The able-bodied have been instructed to get up there and out of harm's way. Once the bombs have taken care of most of the dead, they'll go back in and finish clearing out the last few stragglers."

Out of instinct, I followed them when they reached a larger battleship.

The man called Sharp stopped me before I could enter the conference room.

"Who are you?" he demanded. "I don't recognize your name."

"I need to find someone to turn myself in to," I replied in broken English.

"Oh, good God. I've brought a German into our midst," he groaned. "Stay right there."

Two soldiers took up positions beside me until he could come back with an interpreter.

"Why are you wearing parts of a uniform? Weren't you fighting on our side down there?" He appeared very confused.

"Yes, sir. I escaped the Germans and would like to have asylum. My wife was supposed to bring valuable information to the army, but I have no idea if she made it or not. The man who created those things out there today is a scientist named Rudi Vogel. I'm not sure of the last few adjustments he'd made, but I can give you the plans for where he was only a few weeks ago."

Sharp sighed. "What's your name?"

"Wilhelm Gradl von Boden."

"Boden? Is your wife named Thea?"

"Yes."

"Then I'll take you to the general, who will want to meet you. And when this horrible day is over, maybe they'll let you see your wife and kids."

"They're alive?" I sagged in relief.

"Yes, they are. I'll have someone get you something to eat while you wait. Oh, and I'll need to take that pistol from you."

Eagerly, I took it by the butt and placed it in his hand. "I'm not a threat, I promise. I just want to see my family when it's possible."

"You did good out there today. I think that's the least we can do for you."

Someone called his name, and he hurried off, but I was content to wait, wanting nothing more than to finally be back with my family.

CHAPTER FOURTEEN

CAMERON

These things just would not die. Why wouldn't they stay dead? Oh, wait, someone had messed with their bodies so they wouldn't actually die.

Today had to be the longest day I'd ever known, and it just wouldn't end either.

What had started out with such promise had quickly gone sideways. I'd seen some messed up crap, but these zombie things had to take the cake.

Booth and I had climbed up the cliff for a second time, and all our bodies wanted to do was collapse.

"Whoo!" Booth hollered when we both finally got to the top. "That was amazing. I could do it a couple more times and still be able to go again."

"Ugh," I groaned, working to get my arms and legs moving again. "I hope we can get some rest, or be relieved at some point in the near future."

"Yeah, good luck with that." Anderson pointed to the dead that were pouring around the edge of the mountain and onto the main beach, where most of our men were stationed.

"Let's go kill some dead people." Booth quickly gathered as many men together as he could.

"You're regretting leaving that girl down there, aren't you?" Anderson questioned, as if he could sense my reluctance.

"Yeah. She's something else, and I don't want to lose her." A grin appeared on my face. "I think I just got my second wind. Time to use it."

Getting into position, I crouched along the ridge and took aim.

• • • • ● • ● • • • •

Minutes turned into hours, and time seemed to stretch out indefinitely as I fired. Rinse and repeat.

The only sound I could hear over the rapid fire of our guns was the occasional Messerschitt or Heinkel shooting at us.

Pittman had managed to get a few privates to bring us ammo while we took out some of the dead that were taking a stroll toward our wounded on the beach.

When Booth had gotten the radio call to rain down boulders on their heads to build a stopping place for our troops to regroup, he'd set off to make it happen.

Anderson and I were left behind to continue with the live target practice. When this war was over, I'd be able to win any gun competition I tried out for due to all the practice I was getting in today.

Two new men came and took our spots, but since we could no longer hear, we simply nodded and moved out of their way.

I wasn't even sure we were making a dent in the amount of those who were coming around the mountain. They'd long since made it over the boulders and temporary barricades.

Each line had been able to hold them off for only a short while before losing ground to the massive amounts of our dead who joined them.

My radio buzzed. I pulled it close so I could try to catch what was being said, but only shook my head in frustration as it vibrated in my hand, not hearing a blasted thing they were telling us.

One of the new guys motioned to the sky, informing us they were going to drop bombs shortly for those of us who'd been working for hours to take cover under the newly put together tents and get some rest.

Rest. That word sounded so out of sync with the thought of bombs dropping and the dead moving about, causing more damage than any tank or machine gun could.

I might not be able to sleep, but I could grab an MRE.

Planes swarmed overhead, and I watched as they started bombing the beaches.

Some of our own men were still down there, but at this point, there wasn't much difference between our dead and the dead of the enemy. They were both killers bent on destroying those who were living.

Anderson touched my arm gently and pointed to the tents, but I could barely summon the energy to nod in acknowledgement.

Food had sounded so good only moments before, but the sight of blankets stacked in the corner was the turning point for me. I snagged two, putting one under my head, and the other under my body, pulling the some of it over me.

That was the last coherent thought I had for six hours.

Booth nudged me with his boot.

"Hey, Cameron. You going to sleep all day, or be part of the cleanup crew for the beach?"

I wearily rubbed my eyes. "What are you talking about?"

"You missed all the fun," he cackled with glee. "We bombed the shit out of those guys. We won!"

I stood up and tried to stretch, which only caused my joints to ache more.

Someone had started a pot of coffee, and there was real food being made on portable stoves.

A cup was placed in my hand as I walked out of the tent.

The beach was nothing like I'd last seen it only a short time before.

There were pieces of bodies strewn all over the sand as far as the eye could see, while lines of incoming soldiers were unloading from the boats as wounded were taken on.

The new troops were being sent around the mountain and up a makeshift set of stairs that were shockingly still stable.

A few men worked to place all the body parts into piles, making sure there weren't any survivors under the debris.

It was a nasty job, and I didn't envy any of them.

Anderson arrived at my elbow.

"Did you hear? We all got a field promotion while we were asleep."

"How on earth is that possible?"

"We're all corporals now. They're bringing in new troops, and Pittman has promised to keep us all in the same unit."

"Well, Booth couldn't lead a unit to save his life," I huffed.

Anderson smiled. "That's why the two of us go wherever he does."

"Ah, now the light comes on. Do we know where they're going to send us next?" I couldn't imagine us continuing inland with the dead being made to fight against us.

"We're to rest here and regroup until we're sure those things are a hundred percent dead. The rumor is, this was just a test, and that they don't have more of these things made yet. Since we stopped them, they may decide it wasn't worth the effort." Anderson shrugged, as if it wasn't really his concern.

"If that's the case, then we might just have a chance to win the war. This was a bloody way to find out the Germans might just have outsmarted us."

"They're saying we'll get a visit from the general once things are situated. You'll get to see your girl again."

"Which is great, but how many of our guys won't get to see anyone again?" I questioned.

This whole thing had taken so many lives on both sides, but was it worth the cost of acquiring this little stretch of beach?

Only time would tell if this had been a turning point in the war effort, or just a waste of lives.

EPILOGUE

RUDI

I had been running ever since word that my creations had gotten out of hand and were killing our own men. Without any problems, I'd taken the uniform off of General Otto Adolph so I could easily pass back into Germany. Maybe if I could make it to my home with its secret lab, I would be safe from punishment.

The green grasses of my homeland welcomed me eagerly back into the fold.

My home was empty when I arrived, and I hurried to my office so I could gather anything that might be used against me. I had a few friends left in the Gestapo who would alert me if I was in danger of being taken. So, until then, I was going to close all the access points that would be used to find me.

As the door closed behind me, I turned around, only to run into my apprentice, Karl Müller, the man who was going to betray me.

"Rudi, I'm sorry, but I'm going to have to turn you in. The reward is quite substantial, and will take care of me for years to come as I continue working on what you've begun." He shook his head, as if it was going to bother him greatly for being the cause of my death.

I knew better. He couldn't wait to use me for his own gain. I had always been a means to an end, and my end was going to be his beginning. The stepping stone he'd been working on while I gave him everything he needed to rise above me.

He reached around me to open the door I'd just closed.

"This is Rudi Vogel. You can take him into custody now." He waited for them to reach the front door before he spoke again. "You almost had it all. See you in hell."

The cackle that escaped my lips must have made me sound completely mad. I didn't really care, though, as the situation was so ironic.

I'd created death in a new and interesting way. My research would live on, bringing all sorts of new and exciting types of warfare into the future.

My life's work was continuing without me, and I could have peace with that.

The house's large doors slammed shut behind me, and my guards stopped as I'd moved farther toward the prison truck awaiting me.

This was to be the end. They weren't even going to give me the chance to rot in prison for fear the Allies would find a way to use me for their own deeds.

Shots rang out, and I could feel the impact as they hit my body.

I would have the last word, though.

The syringe slipped from my fingers as I fell to the ground. The change would happen fairly quickly, and I would get my revenge.

"He's bleeding out. Do we need to wait for him to die before we leave?" one of the guards asked as my breath grew raspy.

"We should load him into the truck so they can see the proof that he's dead."

I shook as the serum made its way through my body.

With a growl, they dropped me, but they weren't fast enough to survive my attack.

Even in death, I'd been victorious against my enemies.

• • • ● ● • ● ● • •

Wilhelm and Thea were given asylum in London, where he underwent many tests to find out what had been given to him in the serum by the Germans.

They and their three children returned to Germany at the end of the war to help rebuild their country.

Wilhelm lived to the ripe old age of 75 and was given a merciful death to ensure he wouldn't come back as one of the dead.

Cameron made it through the war, and continued to write letters to Irene until they were able to be married after he retired from the service.

Irene followed in her father's footsteps and continued to work on an antidote that would keep soldiers from rising from the dead. They had five children, to the utter delight of their parents.

The Russians had found a couple of their men wandering around after the battle of Demyansk, and secretly began to run their own tests on the virus.

It wouldn't be discovered until later the exact extent of research the Russians did, but the virus mutated and became viable as a weapon during the Korean War.

If you enjoyed this story, be sure to read what happens to the virus as it erupts during the present day, once again leaving the fate of the world in jeopardy.

Moms Against Zombies readerlinks.com/l/2175433

Do you want to know when the next book comes out or to get to know me better? Sign up for my newsletter and receive a free copy of my short story- Alone Against Zombies.

Or you can stalk me on all the social media sites. (No real-life stalking because that's just not cool.) Thanks for reading, and I hope to hear from you.   -Alathia Morgan

ALSO BY

More Books from Alathia Morgan

Against Zombies Series

Dead Cities Series

Dead in Dallas Book 1

Dead in Denver Book 2

Dead in Detroit Book 3

Infected History
Series

Infected Waters: A Titanic
Disaster Book 1

Infected Poppy Fields: A WWI
Disaster Book 2

Infected Storm Troopers: A
WWII Disaster Book 3

Ghost Ship

Also Writing as Paris Morgan

Murders of the Zodiac

Aquarius Book 1

Pisces Book 2

Secrets and Lies

Poisoned Tales

Writing Romance as Pepper Paris:

Summers of Love

Carter: Summers of Love 1

Kelly: Summers of Love 2

Wade: Summers of Love 3

Jay: Summers of Love 4

Feathered Protectors Series

Fierce Book 1

Flight Book 2

Flicker Book 3

Monsters Under the Bed

Rook Unleashed

Athena

ABOUT AUTHOR

Dr. Pepper is the fuel by which Alathia Morgan's zombie stories are brought to life. While she hopes that she won't have to face her worst fear of being in a real life zombie apocalypse, not having her favorite drink or having electricity to get through it would be horrible.

She enjoys watching her favorite t.v. shows, reading books and quilting while contemplating how to get her characters out of their next life or death set of problems.

She also writes thrillers under the name Paris Morgan and spicy, steamy romances under the name Pepper Paris.

Sign up Here for a free short Against Zombies story and join my Zombie News: Click Now!

https://dl.bookfunnel.com/prnj3oyym7

Author Facebook page:
http://www.facebook.com/apmorganbooks
   Instagram: http://www.instagram.com/alathiamg
   Twitter: http://www.twitter.com/alathiamg
   Street Team:
https://www.facebook.com/groups/1442476186066361/
   Website: http://www.misdirectedtales.com
   Goodreads:
https://www.goodreads.com/author/show/8611387.Alath
ia_Paris_Morgan
   Bookbub:
https://www.bookbub.com/authors/alathia-morgan

Printed in Great Britain
by Amazon

18969768R00108